# The Phantom Tollbooth

## Norton Juster

Illustrated by Jules Feiffer

COLLINS · LIONS

First published 1962 by William Collins Sons and Co Ltd
14 St James's Place, London SW1
First published in Lions 1974

© Text Norman Juster 1961
© Illustrations Jules Feiffer 1961

Printed in Great Britain
by William Collins Sons and Co Ltd, Glasgow

*To Andy and Kenny, who waited so patiently*

# Contents

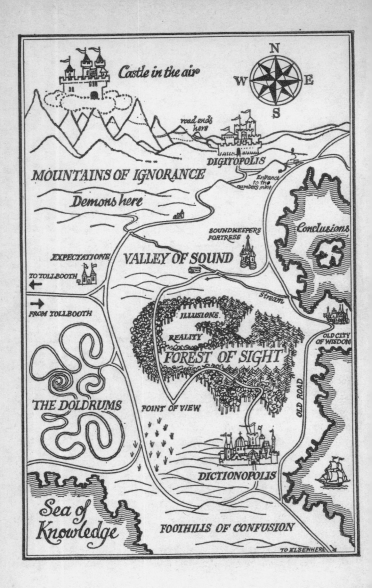

# 1 *Milo*

There was once a boy named Milo who didn't know what to do with himself – not just sometimes, but always.

When he was in school he longed to be out, and when he was out he longed to be in. On the way he thought about coming home, and coming home he thought about going. Wherever he was he wished he was somewhere else, and when he got there he wondered why he'd bothered. Nothing really interested him – least of all the things that should have.

'It seems to me that almost everything is a waste of time,' he remarked one day as he walked dejectedly home from school. 'I can't see the point in learning to solve useless problems, or subtracting turnips from turnips, or knowing where Ethiopia is, or how to spell February.' And, since no one bothered to explain otherwise, he regarded the process of seeking knowledge as the greatest waste of time of all.

As he and his unhappy thoughts hurried along (for while he was never anxious to be where he was going, he liked to get there as quickly as possible) it seemed a great wonder that the world, which was so large, could sometimes feel so small and empty.

'And worst of all,' he continued sadly, 'there's nothing for me to do, nowhere I'd care to go, and hardly anything worth

seeing.' He punctuated this last thought with such a deep sigh that a house sparrow singing near by stopped and rushed home to be with his family.

Without stopping or looking up, he rushed past the buildings and busy shops that lined the street and in a few minutes reached home – dashed through the hall – hopped into the lift – two, three, four, five, six, seven, eight, and off again – opened the door of the flat – rushed into his room – flopped dejectedly into a chair, and grumbled softly, 'Another long afternoon.'

He looked glumly at all the things he owned. The books that were too much trouble to read, the tools he'd never learned to use, the small electric car he hadn't driven for months – or was it years? – and the hundreds of other games and toys, and bats and balls, and bits and pieces scattered around him. And then, on the far side of the room he noticed something he had certainly never seen before.

Who could possibly have left such an enormous package and such a strange one? For, while it was not quite square, it was definitely not round, and for its size it was larger than almost any other big package of smaller dimension that he'd ever seen.

Attached to one side was a bright-blue envelope which said simply: FOR MILO, WHO HAS PLENTY OF TIME.

Of course, if you've ever received a surprise package, you can imagine how puzzled and excited Milo was; and if you've never received one, pay close attention, because some day you might.

'I don't think it's my birthday,' he puzzled, 'and Christmas must be months away, and I haven't been outstandingly good, or even good at all.' (He had to admit this, even to himself.) 'Probably I won't like it anyway, but since I don't know where it came from, I can't possibly send it back.' He thought about it for quite a while and then opened the envelope, but just to be polite.

ONE GENUINE TURNPIKE TOLLBOOTH, it stated – and then it went on:

EASILY ASSEMBLED AT HOME, AND FOR USE BY THOSE WHO HAVE NEVER TRAVELLED IN LANDS BEYOND.

'Beyond what?' thought Milo as he continued to read.

THIS PACKAGE CONTAINS THE FOLLOWING ITEMS:

One (1) genuine turnpike tollbooth to be erected according to directions.

Three (3) precautionary signs to be used in a precautionary fashion.

Assorted coins for use in paying tolls.

One (1) map, up-to-date and carefully drawn by master cartographers, depicting natural and man-made features.

One (1) book of rules and traffic regulations, which may
not be bent or broken.

And in smaller letters at the bottom it concluded:

Results are not guaranteed, but if not perfectly satisfied, your
wasted time will be refunded.

Following the instructions, which told him to cut here, lift
there, and fold back all around, he soon had the tollbooth un-
packed and set up on its stand. He fitted the windows in
place and attached the roof, which extended out on both sides
and fastened on the coin box. It was very much like the toll-
booths he'd seen on family trips, except of course it was much
smaller and purple.

'What a strange present,' he thought to himself. 'The least
they could have done was to send a motorway with it, for it's
terribly impractical without one.' But since, at the time, there
was nothing else he wanted to play with, he set up the three
signs,

**SLOW DOWN APPROACHING TOLLBOOTH**
**PLEASE HAVE YOUR FARE READY**
**HAVE YOUR DESTINATION IN MIND**

and slowly unfolded the map.

As the announcement stated, it was a beautiful map, in
many colours, showing principal roads, rivers, and seas, towns
and cities, mountains and valleys, intersections and detours,
and sites of outstanding interest both beautiful and historic.

The only trouble was that Milo had never heard of any of
the places it indicated, and even the names sounded most
peculiar.

'I don't think there really is such a country,' he concluded
after studying it carefully. 'Well, it doesn't matter anyway.'
And he closed his eyes and poked a finger at the map.

'Dictionopolis,' read Milo slowly when he saw what his

finger had chosen. 'Oh, well, I might as well go there as anywhere.'

He walked across the room and dusted the car carefully. Then, taking the map and rule book with him, he hopped in and, for lack of anything better to do, drove slowly up to the tollbooth. As he deposited his coin and rolled past he remarked wistfully, 'I do hope this is an interesting game, otherwise the afternoon will be so terribly dull.'

Suddenly he found himself speeding along an unfamiliar country road, and as he looked back over his shoulder neither the tollbooth nor his room nor even the house was anywhere in sight. What had started as make-believe was now very real.

'What a strange thing to happen,' he thought (just as you must be thinking). 'This game is much more serious than I thought, for here I am riding on a road I've never seen, going to a place I've never heard of, and all because of a tollbooth which came from nowhere. I'm certainly glad that it's a nice day for a trip,' he concluded hopefully, for, at the moment, this was the one thing he definitely knew.

The sun sparkled, the sky was clear, and all the colours he saw seemed to be richer and brighter than he could ever remember. The flowers shone as if they'd been cleaned and polished, and the tall trees that lined the road shimmered in silvery green.

WELCOME TO EXPECTATIONS, said a carefully lettered sign on a small house at the side of the road.

INFORMATION, PREDICTIONS, AND ADVICE CHEER-FULLY OFFERED. PARK HERE AND BLOW HORN.

With the first sound from the horn a little man in a long

coat came rushing from the house, speaking as fast as he could, and repeating everything several times:

'My, my, my, my, my, welcome, welcome, welcome, welcome to the land of Expectations, to the land of Expectations, to the land of Expectations. We don't get many travellers these days; we certainly don't get many travellers these days. Now what can I do for you? I'm the Whether Man.'

'Is this the right road for Dictionopolis?' asked Milo, a little bowled over by the effusive greeting.

'Well now, well now, well now,' he began again, 'I don't know of any wrong road to Dictionopolis, so if this road goes to Dictionopolis at all it must be the right road, and if it doesn't it must be the right road to somewhere else, because there are no wrong roads to anywhere. Do you think it will rain?'

'I thought you were the Weather Man,' said Milo, very confused.

'Oh no,' said the little man, 'I'm the Whether Man, not the Weather Man, for after all it's more important to know whether there will be weather than what the weather will be.' And with that he released a dozen balloons that sailed off into the sky. 'Must see which way the wind is blowing,' he said, chuckling over his little joke and watching them disappear in all directions.

'What kind of a place is Expectations?' inquired Milo, unable to see the joke and feeling very doubtful of the little man's sanity.

'Good question, good question,' he exclaimed. 'Expectations is the place you must always go to before you get to

where you're going. Of course, some people never go beyond Expectations, but my job is to hurry them along whether they like it or not. Now what else can I do for you?' And before Milo could reply he rushed into the house and reappeared a moment later with a new coat and an umbrella.

'I think I can find my own way,' said Milo, not at all sure that he could. But, since he didn't understand the little man at all, he decided that he might as well move on – at least until he met someone whose sentences didn't always sound as if they would make as much sense backwards as forwards.

'Splendid, splendid, splendid,' exclaimed the Whether Man. 'Whether or not you find your own way, you're bound to find some way. If you happen to find my way, please return it, as it was lost years ago. I imagine by now it's quite rusty. You did say it was going to rain, didn't you?' And with that he opened the umbrella and walked with Milo to the car.

'I'm glad you made your own decision. I do so hate to make up my mind about anything, whether it's good or bad, up or down, in or out, rain or shine. Expect everything, I always say, and the unexpected never happens. Now please drive carefully; good-bye, good-bye, good-bye, good . . .' His last good-bye was drowned out by an enormous clap of thunder, and as Milo drove down the road in the bright sunshine he could see the Whether Man standing in the middle of a fierce cloudburst that seemed to be raining only on him.

The road dipped now into a broad green valley and stretched towards the horizon. The little car bounced along with very little effort, and Milo had hardly to touch the accelerator to go as fast as he wanted. He was glad to be on his way again.

'It's all very well to spend time in Expectations,' he thought, 'but talking to that strange man all day would certainly get me nowhere. He's the most peculiar person I've ever met,' continued Milo – unaware of how many peculiar people he would shortly encounter.

As he drove along the peaceful road he soon fell to day-dreaming and paid less and less attention to where he was going. In a short time he wasn't paying any attention at all, and that is why, at a fork in the road, when a sign pointed to the left, Milo went to the right, along a route which looked suspiciously like the wrong way.

Things began to change as soon as he left the main highway. The sky became quite grey and, along with it, the whole countryside seemed to lose its colour and assume the same monotonous tone. Everything was quiet, and even the air hung heavily. The birds sang only grey songs and the road wound back and forth in an endless series of climbing curves.

Mile after

mile after

mile after

mile he drove, and now, gradually the car went slower and slower, until it was hardly moving at all.

'It looks as though I'm getting nowhere,' yawned Milo, becoming very drowsy and dull. 'I hope I haven't taken a wrong turn.'

Mile after

mile after

mile after

mile, and everything became greyer and more monotonous. Finally, the car just stopped altogether, and, hard as he tried, it wouldn't budge another inch.

'I wonder where I am,' said Milo in a very worried tone.

'You're . . . in . . . the . . . Dol . . . drums,' wailed a voice that sounded far away.

He looked around quickly to see who had spoken. No one was there, and it was as quiet and still as one could imagine.

'Yes . . . the . . . Dol . . . drums,' yawned another voice, but still he saw no one.

'WHAT ARE THE DOLDRUMS?' he cried loudly, and tried very hard to see who would answer this time.

'The Doldrums, my young friend, are where nothing ever happens and nothing ever changes.'

This time the voice came from so close that Milo jumped with surprise, for, sitting on his right shoulder, so lightly that he hardly noticed, was a small creature exactly the colour of his shirt.

'Allow me to introduce all of us,' the creature went on. 'We are the Lethargarians, at your service.'

Milo looked around and, for the first time, noticed dozens of them – sitting on the car, standing in the road, and lying all over the trees and bushes. They were very difficult to see, because whatever they happened to be sitting on or near was exactly the colour they happened to be. Each one looked very much like the other (except for the colour, of course) and

some looked even more like each other than they did like themselves.

'I'm very pleased to meet you,' said Milo, not sure whether or not he was pleased at all. 'I think I'm lost. Can you help me please?'

'Don't say "think",' said one sitting on his shoe, for the one on his shoulder had fallen asleep. 'It's against the law.' And he yawned and fell off to sleep, too.

'No one's allowed to think in the Doldrums,' continued a third, beginning to doze off. And as each one spoke, he fell off to sleep and another picked up the conversation with hardly any interruption.

'Don't you have a rule book? It's local ordinance 175389-J.'

Milo quickly pulled the rule book from his pocket, opened to the page, and read, 'Ordinance 175389-J: It shall be unlawful, illegal, and unethical to think, think of thinking, surmise, presume, reason, meditate, or speculate while in the Doldrums. Anyone breaking this law shall be severely punished!'

'That's a ridiculous law,' said Milo, quite indignantly. 'Everybody thinks.'

'We don't,' shouted the Lethargarians all at once.

'And most of the time *you* don't,' said a yellow one sitting in a daffodil. 'That's why you're here. You weren't thinking, and you weren't paying attention either. People who don't pay attention often get stuck in the Doldrums.' And with that he toppled out of the flower and fell snoring into the grass.

Milo couldn't help laughing at the little creature's strange behaviour, even though he knew it might be rude.

'Stop that at once,' ordered the tartan one clinging to his stocking. 'Laughing is against the law. Don't you have a rule book? It's local ordinance 574381-W.'

Opening the book again, Milo found Ordinance 574381-W: 'In the Doldrums, laughter is frowned upon and smiling is permitted only on alternate Thursdays. Violators shall be dealt with most harshly.'

'Well, if you can't laugh or think, what can you do?' asked Milo.

'Anything as long as it's nothing, and everything as long as it isn't anything,' explained another. 'There's lots to do; we have a very busy schedule –

'At 8 o'clock we get up, and then we spend

'From 8 to 9 daydreaming.

'From 9 to 9.30 we take our early midmorning nap.

'From 9.30 to 10.30 we dawdle and delay.

'From 10.30 to 11.30 we take our late early morning nap.

'From 11.30 to 12.00 we bide our time and then eat lunch.

'From 1.00 to 2.00 we linger and loiter.

'From 2.00 to 2.30 we take our early afternoon nap.

'From 2.30 to 3.30 we put off for tomorrow what we could have done today.

'From 3.30 to 4.00 we take our early late afternoon nap.

'From 4.00 to 5.00 we loaf and lounge until dinner.

'From 6.00 to 7.00 we dilly-dally.

'From 7.00 to 8.00 we take our early evening nap, and then for an hour before we go to bed at 9.00 we waste time.

'As you can see, that leaves almost no time for brooding, lagging, plodding, or procrastinating, and if we stopped to think or laugh, we'd never get nothing done.'

'You mean you'd never get anything done,' corrected Milo.

'We don't want to get anything done,' snapped another angrily; 'we want to get nothing done, and we can do that without your help.'

'You see,' continued another in a more conciliatory tone, 'it's really quite strenuous doing nothing all day, so once a week we take a holiday and go nowhere, which was just where we were going when you came along. Would you care to join us?'

'I might as well,' thought Milo; 'that's where I seem to be going anyway.'

'Tell me,' he yawned, for he felt ready for a nap now himself, 'does everyone here do nothing?'

'Everyone but the terrible watchdog,' said two of them, shuddering in chorus. 'He's always sniffing around to see that nobody wastes time. A most unpleasant character.'

'The watchdog?' said Milo quizzically.

'THE WATCHDOG,' shouted another, fainting from fright, for racing down the road barking furiously and kicking up a great cloud of dust was the very dog of whom they had been speaking.

'RUN!'

'WAKE UP!'

'RUN!'

'HERE HE COMES!'
'THE WATCHDOG!'
Great shouts filled the air as the Lethargarians scattered in
all directions and soon disappeared entirely.

'R-R-R-G-H-R-O-R-R-H-F-F,' exclaimed the watchdog as he
dashed up to the car, loudly puffing and panting.

Milo's eyes opened wide, for there in front of him was a
large dog with a perfectly normal head, four feet, and a tail –
and the body of a loudly ticking alarm-clock.

'What are you doing here?' growled the watchdog.

'Just killing time,' replied Milo apologetically. 'You see –'

'KILLING TIME!' roared the dog – so furiously that his
alarm went off. 'It's bad enough wasting time without killing
it.' And he shuddered at the thought. 'Why are you in the
Doldrums anyway – don't you have anywhere to go?'

'I was on my way to Dictionopolis when I got stuck here,'
explained Milo. 'Can you help me?'

'Help you! You must help yourself,' the dog replied,

carefully winding himself with his left hind leg. 'I suppose you know why you got stuck.'

'I suppose I just wasn't thinking,' said Milo.

'PRECISELY,' shouted the dog as his alarm went off again. 'Now you know what you must do.'

'I'm afraid I don't,' admitted Milo, feeling quite stupid.

'Well,' continued the watchdog impatiently, 'since you got here by not thinking, it seems reasonable to expect that, in order to get out, you must start thinking.' And with that he hopped into the car.

'Do you mind if I get in? I love car rides.'

Milo began to think as hard as he could (which was very difficult, since he wasn't used to it). He thought of birds that swim and fish that fly. He thought of yesterday's lunch and tomorrow's dinner. He thought of words that began with J

and numbers that end in 3. And, as he thought, the wheels began to turn.

'We're moving, we're moving,' he shouted happily.

'Keep thinking,' scolded the watchdog.

The little car started to go faster and faster as Milo's brain whirled with activity, and down the road they went. In a few moments they were out of the Doldrums and back on the main road. All the colours had returned to their original brightness, and as they raced along the road Milo continued to think of all sorts of things; of the many detours and wrong turns that were so easy to take, of how fine it was to be moving along, and, most of all, how much could be accomplished with just a little thought. And the dog, his nose in the wind, just sat back, watchfully ticking.

'You must excuse my gruff conduct,' the watchdog said, after they'd been driving for some time, 'but you see it's traditional for watchdogs to be ferocious . . .'

Milo was so relieved at having escaped the Doldrums that he assured the dog that he bore him no ill-will and, in fact, was very grateful for the assistance.

'Splendid,' shouted the watchdog. 'I'm very pleased – I'm sure we'll be great friends for the rest of the trip. You may call me Tock.'

'That is a strange name for a dog who goes tickticktick-ticktick all day,' said Milo. 'Why didn't they call you –'

'Don't say it,' gasped the dog, and Milo could see a tear well up in his eye.

'I didn't mean to hurt your feelings,' said Milo, not meaning to hurt his feelings.

'That's all right,' said the dog, getting hold of himself. 'It's an old story and a sad one, but I can tell it to you now.

'When my brother was born, the first pup in the family, my parents were overjoyed and immediately named him Tick in expectation of the sound they were sure he'd make. On first winding him, they discovered to their horror that, instead of going tickticktickticktick, he went tocktocktock-tocktocktock. They rushed to the Hall of Records to change the name, but too late. It had already been officially inscribed, and nothing could be done. When I arrived, they were determined not to make the same mistake twice and, since it seemed logical that all their children would make the same sound, they named me Tock. Of course, you know the rest – my brother is called Tick because he goes tocktocktocktocktocktocktock and I am called Tock because I go tickticktickticktickticktick, and both of us are for ever burdened with the wrong names. My parents were so overwrought that they gave up having any more children and devoted their lives to doing good work among the poor and hungry.'

'But how did you become a watchdog?' interjected Milo, hoping to change the subject, as Tock was sobbing quite loudly now.

'That,' he said, rubbing a paw in his eye, 'is also traditional. My family have always been watchdogs – from father to son, almost since time began.

'You see,' he continued, beginning to feel better, 'once there was no time at all, and people found it very inconvenient. They never knew whether they were eating lunch or dinner, and they were always missing trains. So time was invented to help them keep track of the day and get to places when they should. When they began to count all the time that was available, what with 60 seconds in a minute and 60 minutes in an hour and 24 hours in a day and 365 days in a year, it seemed as if there was much more than could ever be used. "If there's so much of it, it couldn't be very valuable," was the general opinion, and it soon fell into disrepute. People wasted it and even gave it away. Then we were given the job of seeing that no one wasted time again,' he said, sitting up proudly. 'It's hard work but a noble calling. For you see' – and now he was standing on the seat, one foot on the wind-screen, shouting with his arms outstretched – 'it is our most valuable possession, more precious than diamonds. It marches on, it and tide wait for no man, and –'

At that point in the speech the car hit a bump in the road and the watchdog collapsed in a heap on the front seat with his alarm again ringing furiously.

'Are you all right?' shouted Milo.

'Umphh,' grunted Tock. 'Sorry to get carried away, but I think you get the point.'

As they drove along, Tock continued to explain the importance of time, quoting the old philosophers and poets and illustrating each point with gestures that brought him perilously close to tumbling headlong from the speeding car.

Before long they saw in the distance the towers and flags of Dictionopolis sparkling in the sunshine, and in a few moments they reached the great wall and stood at the gateway to the city.

'A-H-H-H-R-R-E-M-M-,' roared the sentry, clearing his throat and snapping smartly to attention. 'This is Dictionopolis, a happy kingdom, advantageously located in the Foothills of Confusion and caressed by gentle breezes from the Sea of Knowledge. Today, by royal proclamation, is market-day. Have you come to buy or sell?'

'I beg your pardon?' said Milo.

'Buy or sell, buy or sell,' repeated the sentry impatiently. 'Which is it? You must have come for some reason.'

'Well, I –' Milo began.

'Come now, if you don't have a reason, you must at least have an explanation or certainly an excuse,' interrupted the sentry.

Milo shook his head.

'Very serious, very serious,' the sentry said, shaking his head also. 'You can't get in without a reason.' He thought for a moment, and then continued: 'Wait a minute; maybe I have an old one you can use.'

He took a battered suitcase from the sentry-box and began to rummage busily through it, mumbling to himself, 'No . . . no . . . no . . . this won't do . . . no . . . h-m-m-m . . . ah, this

is fine,' he cried triumphantly, holding up a small medallion on a chain. He dusted it off, and engraved on one side were the words 'WHY NOT?'

'That's a good reason for almost anything – a bit used perhaps, but still quite serviceable.' And with that he placed it around Milo's neck, pushed back the heavy iron gate, bowed low, and motioned them into the city.

'I wonder what the market will be like,' thought Milo as they drove through the gate; but before there was time for an answer they had driven into an immense square crowded with long lines of stalls heaped with merchandise and decorated in gaily coloured bunting. Overhead a large banner proclaimed:

WELCOME TO THE WORLD MARKET

And, from across the square, five very tall, thin gentlemen regally dressed in silks and satins, plumed hats, and buckled shoes rushed up to the car, stopped short, mopped five brows, caught five breaths, unrolled five parchments, and began talking in turn.

'Greetings!'

'Salutations!'

'Welcome!'

'Good afternoon!'

'Hello!'

Milo nodded his head, and they went on, reading from their scrolls.

'By order of Azaz the Unabridged –'

'King of Dictionopolis –'

'Monarch of letters –'

'Emperor of phrases, sentences, and miscellaneous figures of speech –'

'We offer you the hospitality of our kingdom,'

'Country,'

'Nation,'

'State,'

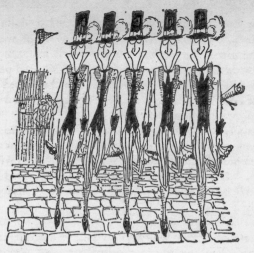

'Commonwealth,'
'Realm,'
'Empire,'
'Palatinate,'
'Principality.'
'Do all those words mean the same thing?' gasped Milo.
'Of course.'
'Certainly.'
'Precisely.'
'Exactly.'
'Yes,' they replied in order.
'Well, then,' said Milo, not understanding why each one said the same thing in a slightly different way, 'wouldn't it be simpler to use just one? It would certainly make more sense.'
'Nonsense.'
'Ridiculous.'
'Fantastic.'
'Absurd.'
'Bosh,' they chorused again, and continued.

'We're not interested in making sense; it's not our job,' scolded the first.

'Besides,' explained the second, 'one word is as good as another – so why not use them all?'

'Then you don't have to choose which one is right,' advised the third.

'Besides,' sighed the fourth, 'if one is right, then ten are ten times as right.'

'Obviously you don't know who we are,' sneered the fifth. And they presented themselves one by one as:

'The Duke of Definition.'

'The Minister of Meaning.'

'The Earl of Essence.'

'The Count of Connotation.'

'The Under-secretary of Understanding.'

Milo acknowledged the introduction and, as Tock growled softly, the minister explained.

'We are the king's advisers, or, in more formal terms, his cabinet.'

'Cabinet,' recited the duke: '(1) a small private room or closet, case with drawers, etc., for keeping valuables or displaying curiosities; (2) council room for chief ministers of state; (3) a body of official advisers to the chief executive of a nation.'

'You see,' continued the minister, bowing thankfully to the duke, 'Dictionopolis is the place where all the words in the world come from. They're grown right here in our orchards.'

'I didn't know that words grew on trees,' said Milo timidly.

'Where did you think they grew?' shouted the earl irritably. A small crowd began to gather to see the little boy who didn't know that letters grew on trees.

'I didn't know they grew at all,' admitted Milo even more timidly. Several people shook their heads sadly.

'Well, money doesn't grow on trees, does it?' demanded the count.

'I've heard not,' said Milo.

'Then something must. Why not words?' exclaimed the under-secretary triumphantly. The crowd cheered his display of logic and continued about its business.

'To continue,' continued the minister impatiently. 'Once a week by Royal Proclamation the world market is held here in the great square, and people come from everywhere to buy the words they need or trade in the words they haven't used.'

'Our job,' said the count, 'is to see that all the words sold are proper ones, for it wouldn't do to sell someone a word that had no meaning or didn't exist at all. For instance, if you bought a word like *ghlbtsk*, where would you use it?'

'It would be difficult,' thought Milo – but there were so many words that were difficult, and he knew hardly any of them.

'But we never choose which ones to use,' explained the earl as they walked towards the market stalls, 'for as long as they mean what they mean to mean we don't care if they make sense or nonsense.'

'Innocence or magnificence,' added the count.

'Reticence or common sense,' said the under-secretary.

'That seems simple enough,' said Milo, trying to be polite.

'Easy as falling off a log,' cried the earl, falling off a log with a loud thump.

'Must you be so clumsy?' shouted the duke.

'All I said was –' began the earl, rubbing his head.

'We heard you,' said the minister angrily, 'and you'll have to find an expression that's less dangerous.'

The earl dusted himself, as the others snickered audibly.

'You see,' cautioned the count, 'you must pick your words very carefully and be sure to say just what you intend to say. And now we must leave to make preparations for the Royal Banquet.'

'You'll be there, of course,' said the minister.

But before Milo had a chance to say anything, they were rushing off across the square as fast as they had come.

'Enjoy yourself in the market,' shouted back the under-secretary.

'Market,' recited the duke: 'an open space or covered building in which –'

And that was the last Milo heard as they disappeared into the crowd.

'I never knew words could be so confusing,' Milo said to Tock as he bent down to scratch the dog's ear.

'Only when you use a lot to say a little,' answered Tock.

Milo thought this was quite the wisest thing he'd heard all day. 'Come,' he shouted, 'let's see the market. It looks very exciting.'

# 4    *Confusion in the Market Place*

Indeed it was, for as they approached, Milo could see crowds of people pushing and shouting their way among the stalls, buying and selling, trading and bargaining. Huge wooden-wheeled carts streamed into the market square from the orchards, and long caravans bound for the four corners of the kingdom made ready to leave. Sacks and boxes were piled high waiting to be delivered to the ships that sailed the Sea of Knowledge, and off to one side a group of minstrels sang songs to the delight of those either too young or too old to engage in trade. But above all the noise and tumult of the crowd could be heard the merchants' voices loudly advertising their products.

'Get your fresh-picked ifs, ands, and buts.'

'Hey-yaa, hey-yaa, hey-yaa, nice ripe wheres and whens.'

'Juicy, tempting words for sale.'

So many words and so many people! They were from every place imaginable and some places even beyond that, and they were all busy sorting, choosing, and stuffing things into cases. As soon as one was filled, another was begun. There seemed to be no end to the bustle and activity.

Milo and Tock wandered up and down between the stalls looking at the wonderful assortment of words for sale. There were short ones and easy ones for everyday use, and long

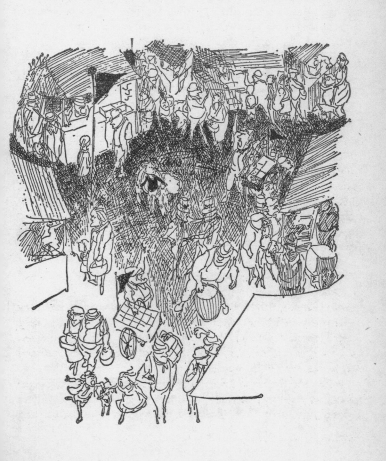

and very important ones for special occasions, and even some marvellously fancy ones packed in individual gift boxes for use in royal decrees and pronouncements.

'Step right up, step right up – fancy, best-quality words right here,' announced one man in a booming voice. 'Step right up – ah, what can I do for you, little boy? How about a nice bagful of pronouns – or maybe you'd like our special assortment of names?'

Milo had never thought much about words before, but these looked so good that he longed to have some.

'Look, Tock,' he cried, 'aren't they wonderful?'

'They're fine, if you have something to say,' replied Tock in a tired voice, for he was much more interested in finding a bone than in shopping for new words.

'Maybe if I buy some I can learn how to use them,' said Milo eagerly as he began to pick through the words in the stall. Finally he chose three which looked particularly good to him – 'quagmire,' 'flabbergast,' and 'upholstery.' He had no idea what they meant, but they looked very grand and elegant.

'How much are these?' he inquired, and when the man whispered the answer he quickly put them back on the shelf and started to walk on.

'Why not take a few pounds of "happys"?' advised the salesman. 'They're much more practical – and very useful for Happy Birthday, Happy New Year, happy days, and happy-go-lucky.'

'I'd like to very much,' began Milo, 'but –'

'Or perhaps you'd be interested in a package of "goods" – always handy for good morning, good afternoon, good evening, and good-bye,' he suggested.

Milo did want to buy something, but the only money he had was the coin he needed to get back through the toll-booth, and Tock, of course, had nothing but the time.

'No, thank you,' replied Milo. 'We're just looking.' And they continued on through the market.

As they turned down the last lane of stalls, Milo noticed a wagon that seemed different from the rest. On its side was a small neatly lettered sign that said DO IT YOURSELF, and inside were twenty-six bins filled with all the letters of the alphabet from A to Z.

'These are for people who like to make their own words,' the man in charge informed him. 'You can pick any assortment you like or buy a special box complete with all letters, punctuation marks, and a book of instructions. Here, taste an A; they're very good.'

Milo nibbled carefully at the letter and discovered that it was quite sweet and delicious – just the way you'd expect an A to taste.

'I knew you'd like it,' laughed the letter man, popping two Gs and an R into his mouth and letting the juice drip down his chin. 'As are one of our most popular letters. All of them aren't so good,' he confided in a low voice. 'Take the Z, for instance – very dry and sawdusty. And the X? Why, it tastes like a trunkful of stale air. That's why people hardly ever use them. But most of the others are quite tasty. Try some more.'

He gave Milo an I, which was icy and refreshing, and Tock a crisp, crunchy C.

'Most people are just too lazy to make their own words,' he continued, 'but it's much more fun.'

'Is it difficult? I'm not much good at making words,' admitted Milo, spitting the pips from a P.

'Perhaps I can be of some assistance – a–s–s–i–s–t–a–n–c–e,' buzzed an unfamiliar voice, and when Milo looked up he saw an enormous bee, at least twice his size, sitting on top of the wagon.

'I am the Spelling Bee,' announced the Spelling Bee. 'Don't be alarmed – a–l–a–r–m–e–d.'

Tock ducked under the wagon, and Milo, who was not over fond of normal-sized bees, began to back away slowly.

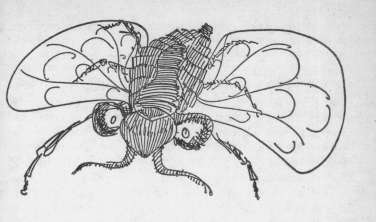

'I can spell anything – a-n-y-t-h-i-n-g,' he boasted, testing his wings. 'Try me, try me!'

'Can you spell good-bye?' suggested Milo as he continued to back away.

The bee gently lifted himself into the air and circled lazily over Milo's head.

'Perhaps – p-e-r-h-a-p-s – you are under the misapprehension – m-i-s-a-p-p-r-e-h-e-n-s-i-o-n – that I am dangerous,' he said, turning a smart loop to the left. 'Let me assure – a-s-s-u-r-e – you that my intentions are peaceful – p-e-a-c-e-f-u-l.' And with that he settled back on top of the wagon and fanned himself with one wing. 'Now,' he panted, 'think of the most difficult word you can and I'll spell it. Hurry up, hurry up!' And he jumped up and down impatiently.

'He looks friendly enough,' thought Milo, not sure just how friendly a friendly bumblebee should be, and tried to think of a very difficult word. 'Spell "vegetable",' he suggested, for it was one that always troubled him at school.

'That is a difficult one,' said the bee, winking at the letter man. 'Let me see now . . . hmmmmmm . . .' He frowned and wiped his brow and paced slowly back and forth on top of the wagon. 'How much time do I have?'

'Just ten seconds,' cried Milo excitedly. 'Count them off, Tock.'

'Oh dear, oh dear, oh dear, oh dear,' the bee repeated, continuing to pace nervously. Then, just as the time ran out, he spelled as fast as he could – 'v-e-g-e-t-a-b-l-e.'

'Correct,' shouted the letter man, and everyone cheered.

'Can you spell everything?' asked Milo admiringly.

'Just about,' replied the bee with a hint of pride in his voice. 'You see, years ago I was just an ordinary bee minding my own business, smelling flowers all day, and occasionally picking up part-time work in people's bonnets. Then one day I realized that I'd never amount to anything without an education and, being naturally adept at spelling, I decided that –'

'BALDERDASH!' shouted a booming voice. And from behind the wagon stepped a large beetle-like insect dressed in a lavish coat, striped trousers, checked waistcoat, spats, and a derby hat. 'Let me repeat – BALDERDASH!' he shouted again, swinging his cane and clicking his heels in mid-air. 'Come now, don't be ill-mannered. Isn't someone going to introduce me to the little boy?'

'This,' said the bee with complete disdain, 'is the Humbug. A very dislikable fellow.'

'NONSENSE! Everyone loves a Humbug,' shouted the Humbug. 'As I was saying to the king just the other day –'

'You've never met the king,' accused the bee angrily. Then, turning to Milo, he said, 'Don't believe a thing this old fraud says.'

'BOSH!' replied the Humbug. 'We're an old and noble family, honourable to the core – *Insecticus Humbugium*, if I

may use the Latin. Why, we fought in the Crusades with Richard the Lion Heart, crossed the Atlantic with Columbus, blazed trails with the pioneers, and today many members of the family hold prominent government positions throughout the world. History is full of Humbugs.'

'A very pretty speech – s-p-e-e-c-h,' sneered the bee. 'Now why don't you go away? I was just advising the lad of the importance of proper spelling.'

'BAH!' said the bug, putting an arm around Milo. 'As soon as you learn to spell one word, they ask you to spell another. You can never catch up – so why bother? Take my advice, my boy, and forget about it. As my great-great-great-grandfather George Washington Humbug used to say –'

'You, sir,' shouted the bee very excitedly, 'are an impostor – i-m-p-o-s-t-o-r – who can't even spell his own name.'

'A slavish concern for the composition of words is the sign of a bankrupt intellect,' roared the Humbug, waving his cane furiously.

Milo didn't have any idea what this meant, but it seemed to infuriate the Spelling Bee, who flew down and knocked off the Humbug's hat with his wing.

'Be careful,' shouted Milo as the bug swung his cane again, catching the bee on the foot and knocking over the box of Ws.

'My foot?' shouted the bee.

'My hat!' shouted the bug – and the fight was on.

The Spelling Bee buzzed dangerously in and out of range of the Humbug's wildly swinging cane as they menaced and threatened each other, and the crowd stepped back out of danger.

'There must be some other way to –' began Milo. And then he yelled, 'WATCH OUT,' but it was too late.

There was a tremendous crash as the Humbug in his great fury tripped into one of the stalls, knocking it into another,

then another, then another, then another, until every stall in the market place had been upset and the words lay scrambled in great confusion all over the square.

The bee, who had tangled himself in some bunting, toppled to the ground, knocking Milo over on top of him, and lay there shouting, 'Help! Help! There's a little boy on me.' The bug sprawled untidily on a mound of squashed letters and Tock, his alarm ringing persistently, was buried under a pile of words.

## 5    *Short Shrift*

'Done what you've looked,' angrily shouted one of the sales-
men. He meant to say 'Look what you've done,' but the
words had got so hopelessly mixed up that no one could make
any sense at all.

'Do going to we what are!' complained another, as everyone set about straightening things up as well as they could.

For several minutes no one spoke an understandable sentence, which added greatly to the confusion. As soon as
possible, however, the stalls were righted and the words swept
into one large pile for sorting.

The Spelling Bee, who was quite upset by the whole affair,
had flown off in a huff, and just as Milo got to his feet the
entire police force of Dictionopolis appeared – loudly blowing
his whistle.

'Now we'll get to the bottom of this,' he heard someone
say. 'Here comes Officer Shrift.'

Striding across the square was the shortest policeman Milo
had ever seen. He was scarcely two feet tall and almost twice
as broad, and he wore a blue uniform with white belt and
gloves, a peaked cap, and a very fierce expression. He continued blowing his whistle until his face was beet red, stopping
only long enough to shout, 'You're guilty, you're guilty,' at
everyone he passed. 'I've never seen anyone so guilty,' he

said as he reached Milo. Then, turning towards Tock, who was still ringing loudly, he said, 'Turn off that dog; it's disrespectful to sound your alarm in the presence of a policeman.'

He made a careful note of that in his black book and strode up and down, his hands clasped behind his back, surveying the wreckage in the market place.

'Very pretty, very pretty.' He scowled. 'Who's responsible for all this? Speak up or I'll arrest the lot of you.'

There was a long silence. Since hardly anybody had actually seen what had happened, no one spoke.

'You,' said the policeman, pointing an accusing finger at the Humbug, who was brushing himself off and straightening his hat, 'you look suspicious to me.'

The startled Humbug dropped his cane and nervously replied, 'Let me assure you, sir, on my honour as a gentleman, that I was merely an innocent bystander, minding my own business, enjoying the stimulating sights and sounds of the world of commerce, when this young lad –'

'AHA!' interrupted Officer Shrift, making another note in his little book. 'Just as I thought: boys are the cause of everything.'

'Pardon me,' insisted the Humbug, 'but I in no way meant to imply that –'

'SILENCE!' thundered the policeman, pulling himself up to full height and glaring menacingly at the terrified bug. 'And now,' he continued, speaking to Milo, 'where were you on the night of 27 July?'

'What does that have to do with it?' asked Milo.

'It's my birthday, that's what,' said the policeman as he entered 'Forgot my birthday' in his little book. 'Boys always forget other people's birthdays.

'You have committed the following crimes,' he continued: 'having a dog with an unauthorized alarm, sowing confusion, upsetting the applecart, wreaking havoc, and mincing words.'

'Now see here,' growled Tock angrily.

'And illegal barking,' he added, frowning at the watchdog. 'It's against the law to bark without using the barking meter. Are you ready to be sentenced?'

'Only a judge can sentence you,' said Milo, who remembered reading that in one of his schoolbooks.

'Good point,' replied the policeman, taking off his cap and putting on a long black robe. 'I am also the judge. Now would you like a long or a short sentence?'

'A short one, if you please,' said Milo.

'Good,' said the judge, rapping his gavel three times. 'I always have trouble remembering the long ones. How about "I am"? That's the shortest sentence I know.'

Everyone agreed that it was a very fair sentence, and the judge continued: 'There will also be a small additional penalty of six million years in prison. Case closed,' he pronounced. 'Come with me. I'll take you to the dungeon.'

'Only a jailer can put you in prison,' offered Milo, quoting the same book.

'Good point,' said the judge, removing his robe and taking out a large bunch of keys. 'I am also the jailer.' And with that he led them away.

'Keep your chin up,' shouted the Humbug. 'Maybe they'll take a million years off for good behaviour.'

The heavy prison door swung back slowly and Milo and Tock followed Officer Shrift down a long dark corridor lit by only an occasional flickering candle.

'Watch the steps,' advised the policeman as they started down a steep circular staircase.

The air was dank and musty – like the smell of wet blankets – and the massive stone walls were slimy to the touch. Down and down they went until they arrived at another door even heavier and stronger-looking than the first. A cobweb brushed across Milo's face and he shuddered.

'You'll find it quite pleasant here,' chuckled the policeman

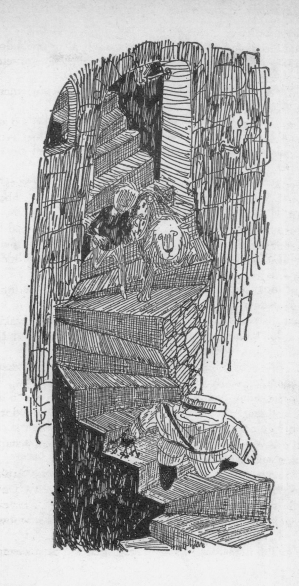

as he slid the bolt back and pushed the door open with a screech and a squeak. 'Not much company, but you can always chat with the witch.'

'The witch?' trembled Milo.

'Yes, she's been here for a long time,' he said, starting along another corridor.

In a few more minutes they had gone through three other doors, across a narrow footbridge, down two more corridors and another stairway, and stood finally in front of a small cell door.

'This is it,' said the policeman. 'All the comforts of home.'

The door opened and then shut and Milo and Tock found themselves in a high vaulted cell with two tiny windows half-way up on the wall.

'See you in six million years,' said Officer Shrift, and the sound of his footsteps grew fainter and fainter until it wasn't heard at all.

'It looks serious, doesn't it, Tock?' said Milo very sadly.

'It certainly does,' the dog replied, sniffing around to see what their new quarters were like.

'I don't know what we're going to do all that time; we don't even have a domino set or a box of crayons.'

'Don't worry,' growled Tock, raising one paw assuringly, 'something will turn up. Here, wind me, will you please? I'm beginning to run down.'

'You know something, Tock?' he said as he wound up the dog. 'You can get in a lot of trouble mixing up words or just not knowing how to spell them. If we ever get out of here, I'm going to make sure to learn all about them.'

'A very commendable ambition, young man,' said a small voice from across the cell.

Milo looked up, very surprised, and noticed for the first time, in the half light of the room, a pleasant-looking old lady quietly knitting and rocking.

'Hello,' he said.

'How do you do?' she replied.

'You'd better be very careful,' Milo advised. 'I understand there's a witch somewhere in here.'

'I am she,' the old lady answered casually, and pulled her shawl a little closer around her shoulders.

Milo jumped back in fright and quickly grabbed Tock to make sure that his alarm didn't go off – for he knew how much witches hate loud noises.

'Don't be frightened,' she laughed. 'I'm not a witch – I'm a Which.'

'Oh,' said Milo, because he couldn't think of anything else to say.

'I'm Faintly Macabre, the not-so-wicked Which,' she continued, 'and I'm certainly not going to harm you.'

'What's a Which?' asked Milo, releasing Tock and stepping a little closer.

'Well,' said the old lady, just as a rat scurried across her foot, 'I am the king's great-aunt. For years and years I was in charge of choosing which words were to be used for all occasions, which ones to say and which ones not to say, which ones to write and which ones not to write. As you can well imagine, with all the thousands to choose from, it was a most important and responsible job. I was given the title of "Official Which", which made me very proud and happy.

'At first I did my best to make sure that only the most proper and fitting words were used. Everything was said clearly and simply and no words were wasted. I had signs posted all over the palace and market place which said:

*Brevity is the Soul of Wit.*

'But power corrupts, and soon I grew miserly and chose fewer and fewer words, trying to keep as many as possible for myself. I had new signs posted which said:

*An Ill-chosen Word is the Fool's Messenger.*

'Soon sales began to fall off in the market. The people were afraid to buy as many words as before, and hard times came to the kingdom. But still I grew more and more miserly. Soon there were so few words chosen that hardly anything could be said, and even casual conversation became difficult. Again I had new signs posted, which said:

*Speak Fitly or be Silent Wisely.*

'And finally I had even these replaced by ones which read simply:
*Silence is Golden.*

'All talk stopped. No words were sold, the market place closed down, and the people grew poor and disconsolate. When the king saw what had happened, he became furious and had me cast into this dungeon where you see me now, an older and wiser woman.

'That was all many years ago,' she continued; 'but they never appointed a new Which, and that explains why today people use as many words as they can and think themselves very wise for doing so. For always remember that while it is wrong to use too few, it is often far worse to use too many.'

When she had finished, she sighed deeply, patted Milo gently on the shoulder, and began knitting once again.

'And have you been down here ever since then?' asked Milo sympathetically.

'Yes,' she said sadly. 'Most people have forgotten me entirely, or remember me wrongly as a witch not a Which. But it matters not, it matters not,' she went on unhappily, 'for they are equally frightened of both.'

'I don't think you're frightening,' said Milo, and Tock wagged his tail in agreement.

'I thank you very much,' said Faintly Macabre. 'You may call me Aunt Faintly. Here, have a punctuation mark.' And

she held out a box of sugar-coated question marks, periods, commas, and exclamation points. 'That's all I get to eat now.'

'Well, when I get out of here, I'm going to help you,' Milo declared forcefully.

'That's very nice of you,' she replied; 'but the only thing that can help me is the return of Rhyme and Reason.'

'The return of what?' asked Milo.

'Rhyme and Reason,' she repeated; 'but that's another long story, and you may not want to hear it.'

'We would like to very much,' barked Tock.

'We really would,' agreed Milo, and as the Which rocked slowly back and forth she told them this story.

# 6 *Faintly Macabre's Story*

'Once upon a time, this land was a barren and frightening wilderness whose high rocky mountains sheltered the evil winds and whose barren valleys offered hospitality to no man. Few things grew, and those that did were bent and twisted and their fruit was as bitter as wormwood. What wasn't waste was desert, and what wasn't desert was rock, and the demons of darkness made their home in the hills. Evil creatures roamed at will through the countryside and down to the sea. It was known as the land of Null.

'Then one day a small ship appeared on the Sea of Knowledge. It carried a young prince seeking the future. In the name of goodness and truth he laid claim to all the country and set out to explore his new domain. The demons, monsters, and giants were furious at his presumption and banded together to drive him out. The earth shook with their battle, and when they had finished, all that remained to the prince was a small piece of land at the edge of the sea.

' "I'll build my city here," he declared, and that is what he did.

'Before long, more ships came bearing settlers for the new land and the city grew and pushed its boundaries farther and farther out. Each day it was attacked anew, but nothing could destroy the prince's new city. And grow it did. Soon it was no longer just a city; it was a kingdom, and it was called the kingdom of Wisdom.

'But, outside the walls, all was not safe, and the new king vowed to conquer the land that was rightfully his. So each spring he set forth with his army and each autumn he returned, and year by year the kingdom grew larger and more prosperous. He took to himself a wife and before long had two fine young sons to whom he taught everything he knew so that one day they might rule wisely.

'When the boys grew to young manhood, the king called them to him and said: "I am becoming an old man and can no longer go forth to battle. You must take my place and found new cities in the wilderness, for the kingdom of Wisdom must grow."

'And so they did. One went south to the Foothills of Confusion and built Dictionopolis, the city of words; and one went north to the Mountains of Ignorance and built Digitopolis, the city of numbers. Both cities flourished mightily and the demons were driven back still farther. Soon other cities and towns were founded in the new lands, and at last only the farthest reaches of the wilderness remained to these terrible creatures – and there they waited, ready to strike down all who ventured near or relaxed their guard.

'The two brothers were glad, however, to go their separate ways, for they were by nature very suspicious and jealous. Each one tried to outdo the other, and they worked so hard and diligently at it that before long their cities rivalled even Wisdom in size and grandeur.

' "Words are more important than wisdom," said one privately.

' "Numbers are more important than wisdom," thought the other to himself.

'And they grew to dislike each other more and more.

'The old king, however, who knew nothing of his sons' animosity, was very happy in the twilight of his reign and spent his days quietly walking and contemplating in the royal gardens. His only regret was that he'd never had a daughter, for he loved little girls as much as he loved little boys. One day as he was strolling peacefully about the grounds, he discovered two tiny babies that had been abandoned in a basket under the grape arbour. They were beautiful golden-haired girls.

'The king was overjoyed. "They have been sent to crown my old age," he cried, and called the queen, his ministers, the palace staff, and, indeed, the entire population to see them.

' "We'll call this one Rhyme and this one Reason," he said, and so they became the Princess of Sweet Rhyme and the Princess of Pure Reason and were brought up in the palace.

'When the old king finally died, the kingdom was divided between his two sons, with the provision that they would be equally responsible for the welfare of the young princesses. One son went south and became Azaz, the unabridged king of Dictionopolis, and the other went north and became the Mathemagician, ruler of Digitopolis; and, true to their words, they both provided well for the little girls, who continued to live in Wisdom.

'Everyone loved the princesses because of their great beauty, their gentle ways, and their ability to settle all controversies fairly and reasonably. People with problems or grievances or arguments came from all over the land to seek advice, and even the two brothers, who by this time were

fighting continuously, often called upon them to help decide matters of State. It was said by everyone that "Rhyme and Reason answer all problems."

'As the years passed, the two brothers grew farther and farther apart and their separate kingdoms became richer and grander. Their disputes, however, became more and more difficult to reconcile. But always, with patience and love, the princesses set things right.

'Then one day they had the most terrible quarrel of all. King Azaz insisted that words were far more significant than numbers and hence his kingdom was truly the greater and the Mathemagician claimed that numbers were much more important than words and hence his kingdom was supreme. They discussed and debated and raved and ranted until they were on the verge of blows, when it was decided to submit the question to arbitration by the princesses.

'After days of careful consideration, in which all the evidence was weighed and all the witnesses heard, they made their decision:

' "Words and numbers are of equal value, for, in the cloak of knowledge, one is warp and the other woof. It is no more important to count the sands than it is to name the stars. Therefore, let both kingdoms live in peace."

'Everyone was pleased with the verdict. Everyone, that is, but the brothers, who were beside themselves with anger.

' "What good are these girls if they cannot settle an argument in someone's favour?" they growled, since both were more interested in their own advantage than in the truth. "We'll banish them from the kingdom for ever."

'And so they were taken from the palace and sent far away to the Castle in the Air, and they have not been seen since. That is why today, in all this land, there is neither Rhyme nor Reason.'

'And what happened to the two rulers?' asked Milo.

'Banishing the two princesses was the last thing they ever agreed upon, and they soon fell to warring with each other. Despite this, their own kingdoms have continued to prosper, but the old city of Wisdom has fallen into great disrepair, and there is no one to set things right. So, you see, until the princesses return, I shall have to stay here.'

'Maybe we can rescue them,' said Milo as he saw how sad the Which looked.

'Ah, that would be difficult,' she replied. 'The Castle in the Air is far from here, and the one stairway which leads to it is guarded by fierce and black-hearted demons.'

Tock growled ominously, for he hated even the thought of demons.

'I'm afraid there's not much a little boy and a dog can do,' she said, 'but never you mind; it's not so bad. I've grown quite used to it here. But you must be going or else you'll waste the whole day.'

'Oh, we're here for six million years,' sighed Milo, 'and I don't see any way to escape.'

'Nonsense,' scolded the Which, 'you mustn't take Officer Shrift so seriously. He loves to put people in prison, but he doesn't care about keeping them there. Now just press that button in the wall and be on your way.'

Milo pressed the button and a door swung open, letting in a shaft of brilliant sunshine.

'Good-bye; come again,' shouted the Which as they stepped outside and the door slammed shut.

Milo and Tock stood blinking in the bright light and, as their eyes became accustomed to it, the first things they saw were the king's advisers again rushing towards them.

'Ah, there you are.'

'Where have you been?'

'We've been looking all over for you.'

'The Royal Banquet is about to begin.'

'Come with us.'

They seemed very agitated and out of breath as Milo walked along with them.

'But what about my car?' he asked.

'Don't need it,' replied the duke.

'No use for it,' said the minister.

'Superfluous,' advised the count.

'Unnecessary,' stated the earl.

'Uncalled for,' cried the under-secretary. 'We'll take our vehicle.'

'Conveyance.'

'Rig.'

'Charabanc.'

'Chariot.'

'Buggy.'

'Coach.'

'Brougham.'

'Shandrydan,' they repeated quickly in order, and pointed to a small wooden wagon.

'Oh dear, all those words again,' thought Milo as he

climbed into the wagon with Tock and the cabinet members. 'How are you going to make it move? It doesn't have a –'

'Be very quiet,' advised the duke, 'for it goes without saying.'

And, sure enough, as soon as they were all quite still, it began to move quickly through the streets, and in a very short time they arrived at the royal palace.

# 7     *The Royal Banquet*

'Right this way.'

'Follow us.'

'Come along.'

'Step lively.'

'Here we go,' they shouted, hopping from the wagon and pounding up the broad marble staircase. Milo and Tock followed close behind. It was a strange-looking palace, and if he didn't know better he would have said that it looked exactly like an enormous book, standing on end, with its front door in the lower part of the binding just where they usually place the publisher's name.

Once inside, they hurried down a long hallway, which glittered with crystal chandeliers and echoed with their footsteps. The walls and ceiling were covered with mirrors, whose reflections danced dizzily along with them, and the footmen bowed coldly.

'We must be terribly late,' gasped the earl nervously as they reached the tall doors of the banquet hall.

It was a vast room, full of people loudly talking and arguing. The long table was carefully set with gold plates and linen napkins. An attendant stood behind each chair, and at the centre, raised slightly above the others, was a throne covered in crimson cloth. Directly behind, on the wall, was the royal coat of arms, flanked by the flags of Dictionopolis.

Milo noticed many of the people he had seen in the market place. The letter man was busy explaining to an interested group the history of the W, and off in a corner the Humbug and the Spelling Bee were arguing fiercely about nothing at all. Officer Shrift wandered through the crowd, suspiciously muttering, 'Guilty, guilty, they're all guilty,' and, on noticing Milo, brightened visibly and commented in passing, 'Is it six million years already? My, how time flies.'

Everyone seemed quite grumpy about having to wait for lunch, and they were all relieved to see the tardy guests arrive.

'Certainly glad you finally made it, old man,' said the Humbug, cordially pumping Milo's hand. 'As guest of honour you must choose the menu of course.'

'Oh, my,' he thought, not knowing what to say.

'Be quick about it,' suggested the Spelling Bee. 'I'm famished – f-a-m-i-s-h-e-d.'

As Milo tried to think, there was an ear-shattering blast of trumpets, entirely off key, and a page announced to the startled guests:

'KING AZAZ THE UNABRIDGED.'

The king strode through the door and over to the table and settled his great bulk on to the throne, calling irritably, 'Places, everyone. Take your places.'

He was the largest man Milo had ever seen, with a great stomach, large piercing eyes, a grey beard that reached to his waist, and a silver signet ring on the little finger of his left hand. He also wore a small crown and a robe with the letters of the alphabet beautifully embroidered all over it.

'What have we here?' he said, staring down at Tock and Milo as everyone else took his place.

'If you please,' said Milo, 'my name is Milo and this is Tock. Thank you very much for inviting us to your banquet, and I think your palace is beautiful.'

'Exquisite,' corrected the duke.

'Lovely,' counselled the minister.

'Handsome,' recommended the count.

'Pretty,' hinted the earl.

'Charming,' submitted the under-secretary.

'SILENCE,' suggested the king. 'Now, young man, what can you do to entertain us? Sing songs? Tell stories? Compose sonnets? Juggle plates? Do tumbling tricks? Which is it?'

'I can't do any of those things,' admitted Milo.

'What an ordinary little boy,' commented the king. 'Why, my cabinet members can do all sorts of things. The duke here can make mountains out of molehills. The minister splits hairs. The count makes hay while the sun shines. The earl leaves no stone unturned. And the under-secretary,' he finished ominously, 'hangs by a thread. Can't you do anything at all?'

'I can count to a thousand,' offered Milo.

'A-A-R-G-H, numbers! Never mention numbers here. Only use them when we absolutely have to,' growled Azaz disgustedly. 'Now, why don't you and Tock come up here and sit next to me, and we'll have some dinner?'

'Are you ready with the menu?' reminded the Humbug.

'Well,' said Milo, remembering that his mother had always told him to eat lightly when he was a guest, 'why don't we have a light meal?'

'A light meal it shall be,' roared the bug, waving his arms.

The waiters rushed in carrying large serving platters and set them on the table in front of the king. When he lifted the

covers, shafts of brilliant-coloured light leaped from the plates and bounced around the ceiling, the walls, across the floor, and out the windows.

'Not a very substantial meal,' said the Humbug, rubbing his eyes, 'but quite an attractive one. Perhaps you can suggest something a little more filling.'

The king clapped his hands, the platters were removed, and, without thinking, Milo quickly suggested, 'Well, in that case, I think we ought to have a square meal of –'

'A square meal it is,' shouted the Humbug again. The king clapped his hands once more and the waiters reappeared

carrying plates heaped high with steaming squares of all sizes and colours.

'Ugh,' said the Spelling Bee, tasting one, 'these are awful.'

No one else seemed to like them very much either, and the Humbug got one caught in his throat and almost choked.

'Time for the speeches,' announced the king as the plates were again removed and everyone looked glum. 'You first,' he commanded, pointing to Milo.

'Your Majesty, ladies and gentlemen,' started Milo timidly, 'I would like to take this opportunity to say that in all the –'

'That's quite enough,' snapped the king. 'Mustn't take all day.'

'But I'd just begun,' objected Milo.

'NEXT!' bellowed the king.

'Roast turkey, mashed potatoes, vanilla ice cream,' recited the Humbug, bouncing up and down quickly.

'What a strange speech,' thought Milo, for he'd heard many

in the past and knew that they were supposed to be long and dull.

'Fish and chips, raspberry jelly, chocolate pudding – p-u-d-d-i-n-g,' said the Spelling Bee in his turn.

'Tomato soup, sausages, strawberry jam,' shouted Officer Shrift from his chair. Since he was taller sitting than standing, he didn't bother to get up.

And so down the line it went, with each guest rising briefly, making a short speech, and then resuming his place. When everyone had finished, the king rose.

'Pâté de foie gras, soupe à l'oignon, faisan sous cloche, salade endive, fromages et fruits et demi-tasse,' he said carefully and clapped his hands again.

The waiters reappeared immediately, carrying heavy, hot trays, which they set on the table. Each one contained the exact words spoken by the various guests, and they all began eating immediately with great gusto.

'Dig in,' said the king, poking Milo with his elbow and looking disapprovingly at his plate. 'I can't say that I think much of your choice.'

'I didn't know that I was going to have to eat my words,' objected Milo.

'Of course, of course, everyone here does,' the king grunted. 'You should have made a tastier speech.'

Milo looked around at everyone busily stuffing himself and then back at his own unappetizing plate. It certainly didn't look worth eating, and he was so very hungry.

'Here, try some somersault,' suggested the duke. 'It improves the flavour.'

'Have a rigmarole,' offered the count, passing the bread-basket.

'Or a ragamuffin,' seconded the minister.

'Perhaps you'd care for a synonym bun,' suggested the duke.

'Why not wait for your just desserts?' mumbled the earl indistinctly, his mouth full of food.

'How many times must I tell you not to bite off more than you can chew?' snapped the under-secretary, patting the distressed earl on the back.

'In one ear and out the other,' scolded the duke, attempting to stuff one of his words through the earl's head.

'If it isn't one thing, it's another,' chided the minister.

'Out of the frying pan into the fire,' shouted the count, burning himself badly.

'Well, you don't have to bite my head off,' screamed the terrified earl, and flew at the others in a rage.

The five of them scuffled wildly under the table.

'STOP THAT AT ONCE,' thundered Azaz, 'or I'll banish the lot of you!'

'Sorry.'

'Excuse me.'

'Forgive us.'

'Pardon.'

'Regrets,' they apologized in turn, and sat down glaring at each other.

The rest of the meal was finished in silence until the king, wiping the gravy stains from his vest, called for dessert. Milo, who had not eaten anything, looked up eagerly.

'We're having a special treat today,' said the king as the delicious smells of home-made pastry filled the banquet hall. 'By royal command the pastry chefs have worked all night in the half bakery to make sure that –'

'The half bakery?' questioned Milo.

'Of course, the half bakery,' snapped the king. 'Where do you think half-baked ideas come from? Now, please don't interrupt. By royal command the pastry chefs have worked all night to –'

'What's a half-baked idea?' asked Milo again.

'Will you be quiet?' growled Azaz angrily; but, before he could begin again, three large serving carts were wheeled into the hall and everyone jumped up to help himself.

'They're very tasty,' explained the Humbug, 'but they don't always agree with you. Here's one that's very good.' He handed it to Milo and, through the icing and nuts, Milo saw that it said THE EARTH IS FLAT.

'People swallowed that one for years,' commented the Spelling Bee, 'but it's not very popular these days – d-a-y-s.' He picked up a long one that stated THE MOON IS MADE OF GREEN CHEESE and hungrily bit off the part that said CHEESE. 'Now *there's* a half-baked idea,' he said, smiling.

Milo looked at the great assortment of cakes, which were being eaten almost as quickly as anyone could read them. The count was munching contentedly on IT NEVER RAINS BUT IT POURS and the king was busy slicing one that stated NIGHT AIR IS BAD AIR.

'I wouldn't eat too many of those if I were you,' advised Tock. 'They may look good, but you can get terribly sick of them.'

'Don't worry,' Milo replied; 'I'll just wrap one up for later,' and he folded his napkin around EVERYTHING HAPPENS FOR THE BEST.

79

'Couldn't eat another thing,' puffed the duke, clutching his stomach.

'Oh my, oh dear,' agreed the minister, breathing with great difficulty.

'M-m-m-m-f-f-m-m,' mumbled the earl, desperately try-ing to swallow another mouthful.

'Thoroughly stuffed,' sighed the count, loosening his belt.

'Full up,' grunted the under-secretary, reaching for the last cake.

As every one finished, the only sounds to be heard were the creaking of chairs, the pushing of plates, the licking of spoons, and, of course, a few words from the Humbug.

'A delightful repast, delicately prepared and elegantly served,' he announced to no one in particular. 'A feast of rare bouquet. My compliments to the chef, by all means; my compliments to the chef.' Then, with a most distressed look on his face, he turned to Milo and gasped, 'Would you kindly fetch me a glass of water? I seem to have a touch of indiges-tion.'

'Perhaps you've eaten too much too quickly,' Milo re-marked sympathetically.

'Too much too quickly, too much too quickly,' wheezed the uncomfortable bug, between gulps. 'To be sure, too much

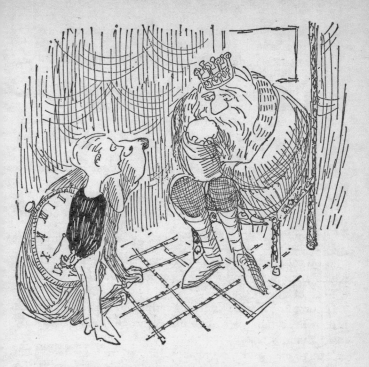

too quickly. I most certainly should have eaten too little too slowly, or too much too slowly, or too little too quickly, or taken all day to eat nothing, or eaten everything in no time at all, or occasionally eaten something any time, or perhaps I should have –' And he toppled back, exhausted, into his chair and continued to mumble indistinctly.

'Attention! Let me have your attention!' insisted the king, leaping to his feet and pounding the table. The command was entirely unnecessary, for the moment he began to speak everyone but Milo, Tock, and the distraught bug rushed from the hall, downstairs, and out of the palace.

'Loyal subjects and friends,' continued Azaz, his voice

echoing in the almost empty room, 'once again on this gala •
occasion we have –'

'Pardon me,' coughed Milo as politely as possible, 'but
everyone has gone.'

'I was hoping no one would notice,' said the king sadly.
'It happens every time.'

'They've all gone to dinner,' announced the Humbug
weakly, 'and just as soon as I catch my breath I shall join
them.'

'That's ridiculous. How can they eat dinner right after a
banquet?' said Milo.

'SCANDALOUS!' shouted the king. 'We'll put a stop to it
at once. From now on, by royal command, everyone must
eat dinner before the banquet.'

'But that's just as bad,' protested Milo.

'You mean just as good,' corrected the Humbug. 'Things
which are equally bad are also equally good. Try to look at
the bright side of things.'

'I don't know which side of anything to look at,' protested
Milo. 'Everything is so confusing and all your words only
make things worse.'

'How true,' said the unhappy king, resting his regal chin
on his royal fist as he thought fondly of the old days. 'There
must be something we can do about it.'

'Pass a law,' the Humbug suggested brightly.

'We have almost as many laws as words,' grumbled the
king.

'Offer a reward,' offered the bug again.

The king shook his head and looked sadder and sadder.

'Send for help.'

'Drive a bargain.'

'Pull the switch.'

'File a brief.'

'Lower the boom.'

'Toe the line.'

'Raise the bridge.'

'Bar the door,' shouted the bug, jumping up and down and waving his arms. Then he promptly sat down as the king glanced furiously in his direction.

'Perhaps you might allow Rhyme and Reason to return,' said Milo softly, for he had been waiting for just such an opportunity to suggest it.

'How nice that would be,' said Azaz, straightening up and adjusting his crown. 'Even if they were a bother at times, things always went so well when they were here.' As he spoke he leaned back on the throne, clasped his hands behind his head, and stared thoughtfully at the ceiling. 'But I'm afraid it can't be done.'

'Certainly not; it can't be done,' repeated the Humbug.

'Why not?' asked Milo.

'Why not indeed?' exclaimed the bug, who seemed equally at home on either side of an argument.

'Much too difficult,' replied the king.

'Of course,' emphasized the bug, 'much too difficult.'

'You could if you really wanted to,' insisted Milo.

'By all means, if you really wanted to, you could,' the Humbug agreed.

'How?' asked Azaz, glaring at the bug.

'How?' inquired Milo, looking the same way.

'A simple task,' began the Humbug, suddenly wishing he were somewhere else, 'for a brave lad with a stout heart, a steadfast dog, and a serviceable small automobile.'

'Go on,' commanded the king.

'Yes, please,' seconded Milo.

'All that he would have to do,' continued the worried bug, 'is travel through miles of harrowing and hazardous countryside, into unknown valleys and uncharted forests, past yawning chasms and trackless wastes, until he reached Digitopolis (if, of course, he ever reached there). Then he would have to persuade the Mathemagician to agree to release the little princesses – and, of course, he'd never agree to agree to anything that you agreed with. And, anyway, if he did, you certainly wouldn't agree to it.

'From there it's a simple matter of entering the Mountains of Ignorance, full of perilous pitfalls and ominous overtones – a land to which many venture but few return, and whose evil demons slither from peak to peak in search of prey. Then an effortless climb up a two-thousand-step circular stairway without railings in a high wind at night (for in those mountains it is always night) to the Castle in the Air.'

He paused momentarily for breath, then began again.

'After a pleasant chat with the princesses, all that remains is a leisurely ride back through those chaotic crags whose frightening fiends have sworn to tear any intruder limb from limb and devour him down to his belt buckle.

'And, finally, after the long ride back, a triumphal parade (if, of course, there is anything left to parade) followed by hot chocolate and cakes for everyone.' The Humbug bowed low and sat down once again, very pleased with himself.

'I never realized it would be so simple,' said the king, stroking his beard and smiling broadly.

'Quite simple indeed,' concurred the bug.

'It sounds dangerous to me,' said Milo.

'Most dangerous, most dangerous,' mumbled the Humbug, still trying to be in agreement with everybody.

'Who will make the journey?' asked Tock, who had been listening very carefully to the Humbug's description.

'A very good question,' replied the king. 'But there is one far more serious problem.'

'What is it?' asked Milo, who was rather unhappy at the turn the conversation had taken.

'I'm afraid I can tell you that only when you return,' cried the king, clapping his hands three times. As he did so the waiters rushed back into the room and quickly cleared away the dishes, the silver, the tablecloth, the table, the chairs, the banquet hall, and the palace, leaving them all suddenly standing in the market-place.

'Of course you realize that I would like to make the trip myself,' continued Azaz, striding across the square as if nothing had happened; 'but, since it was your idea, you shall have all the honour and fame.'

'But you see –' began Milo.

'Dictionopolis will always be grateful, my boy,' interrupted the king, throwing one arm around Milo and patting Tock with the other. 'You will face many dangers on your journey, but fear not, for I have brought you this for your protection.'

He drew from inside his cape a small heavy box about the size of a school book and handed it ceremoniously to Milo.

'In this box are all the words I know,' he said. 'Most of them you will never need, some you will use constantly, but with them you may ask all the questions which have never been answered and answer all the questions which have never been asked. All the great books of the past and all the ones yet to come are made with these words. With them there is no obstacle you cannot overcome. All you must learn to do is use them well and in the right places.'

Milo accepted the gift with thanks and the little group walked to the car, still parked at the edge of the square.

'You will, of course, need a guide,' said the king, 'and, since he knows the obstacles so well, the Humbug has cheerfully volunteered to accompany you.'

'Now see here!' cried the startled bug, for that was the last thing in the world he wanted to do.

'You will find him dependable, brave, resourceful, and loyal,' continued Azaz, and the Humbug was so overcome by the flattery that he quite forgot to object again.

'I'm sure he'll be a great help,' cried Milo as they drove across the square.

'I hope so,' thought Tock to himself, for he was far less sure.

'Good luck, good luck; do be careful,' shouted the king, and down the road they went.

Milo and Tock wondered what strange adventures lay ahead. The Humbug speculated on how he'd ever become involved in such a hazardous undertaking. And the crowd waved and cheered wildly, for, while they didn't care at all about anyone arriving, they were always very pleased to see someone go.

# 9    *It all depends How You Look at Things*

Soon all traces of Dictionopolis had vanished in the distance and all those strange and unknown lands that lay between the kingdom of words and the kingdom of numbers stretched before them. It was late afternoon and the dark-orange sun floated heavily over the distant mountains. A friendly, cool breeze slapped playfully at the car, and the long shadows stretched out lazily from the trees and bushes.

'Ah, the open road!' exclaimed the Humbug, breathing deeply, for he now seemed happily resigned to the trip. 'The spirit of adventure, the lure of the unknown, the thrill of a gallant quest. How very grand indeed.' Then, pleased with himself, he folded his arms, sat back, and left it at that.

In a few more minutes they had left the open countryside and driven into a dense forest.

THIS IS THE SCENIC ROUTE: STRAIGHT AHEAD TO POINT OF VIEW

announced a rather large road sign; but, contrary to its statement, all that could be seen were more trees. As the car rushed along, the trees grew thicker and taller and leafier until just as they'd hidden the sky completely, the forest abruptly ended and the road bent itself around a broad promontory. Stretching below, to the left, the right, and straight ahead, as far as anyone could see, lay the rich green landscape through which they had been travelling.

'Remarkable view,' announced the Humbug, bouncing from the car as if he were responsible for the whole thing.

'Isn't it beautiful?' gasped Milo.

'Oh, I don't know,' answered a strange voice. 'It all depends how you look at things.'

'I beg your pardon?' said Milo, for he didn't see who had spoken.

'I said it depends how you look at things,' repeated the voice.

Milo turned around and found himself staring at two very neatly polished brown shoes, for standing directly in front of him (if you can use the word 'standing' for anyone suspended in mid-air) was another boy just about his age, whose feet were easily three feet off the ground.

'For instance,' continued the boy, 'if you happened to like deserts, you might not think this was beautiful at all.'

'That's true,' said the Humbug, who didn't like to contradict anyone whose feet were so far off the ground.

'For instance,' said the boy again, 'if Christmas trees were people and people were Christmas trees, we'd all be chopped down, put up in the living-room, and covered with tinsel, while the trees opened our presents.'

'What does that have to do with it?' asked Milo.

'Nothing at all,' he answered, 'but it's an interesting possibility, don't you think?'

'How do you manage to stand up there?' asked Milo, for this was the subject which most interested him.

'I was about to ask you a similar question,' answered the boy, 'for you must be much older than you look to be standing on the ground.'

'What do you mean?' Milo asked.

'Well,' said the boy, 'in my family everyone is born in the air, with his head at exactly the height it's going to be when

he's an adult, and then we all grow towards the ground. When we're fully grown up or, as you can see, grown down, our feet finally touch. Of course, there are a few of us whose feet never reach the ground no matter how old we get, but I suppose it's the same in every family.'

He hopped a few steps in the air, skipped back to where he started, and then began again.

'You certainly must be very old to have reached the ground already.'

'Oh no,' said Milo seriously. 'In my family we all start on the ground and grow up, and we never know how far until we actually get there.'

'What a silly system.' The boy laughed. 'Then your head keeps changing its height and you always see things in a different way? Why, when you're fifteen things won't look at all the way they did when you were ten, and at twenty everything will change again.'

'I suppose so,' replied Milo, for he had never really thought about the matter.

'We always see things from the same angle,' the boy continued. 'It's much less trouble that way. Besides, it makes more sense to grow down and not up. When you're very young, you can never hurt yourself falling down if you're in mid-air, and you certainly can't get into trouble for scuffling up your shoes or marking the floor if there's nothing to scuff them on and the floor is three feet away.'

'That's very true,' thought Tock, who wondered how the dogs in the family liked the arrangement.

'But there are many other ways to look at things,' remarked the boy. 'For instance, you had orange juice, boiled eggs, toast and jam, and milk for breakfast,' he said, turning to Milo. 'And you are always worried about people wasting time,' he said to Tock. 'And you are almost never right about anything,' he said, pointing at the Humbug, 'and, when you are, it's usually an accident.'

'A gross exaggeration,' protested the furious bug, who didn't realize that so much was visible to the naked eye.

'Amazing,' gasped Tock.

'How do you know all that?' asked Milo.

'Simple,' he said proudly. 'I'm Alec Bings; I see through things. I can see whatever is inside, behind, around, covered by or subsequent to anything else. In fact, the only thing I can't see is whatever happens to be right in front of my nose.'

'Isn't that a little inconvenient?' asked Milo, whose neck was becoming quite stiff from looking up.

'It is a little,' replied Alec, 'but it is quite important to know what lies behind things, and the family helps me take care of the rest. My father sees to things, my mother looks after things, my brother sees beyond things, my uncle sees the other side of every question, and my little sister Alice sees under things.'

'How can she see under things if she's all the way up there?' growled the Humbug.

'Well,' added Alec, turning a neat cartwheel, 'whatever she can't see under, she overlooks.'

'Would it be possible for me to see something from up there?' asked Milo politely.

'You could,' said Alec, 'but only if you try very hard to look at things as an adult does.'

Milo tried as hard as he could, and, as he did, his feet floated slowly off the ground until he was standing in the air next to Alec Bings. He looked around very quickly and, an instant later, crashed back down to earth again.

'Interesting, wasn't it?' asked Alec.

'Yes, it was,' agreed Milo, rubbing his head and dusting himself off, 'but I think I'll continue to see things as a child. It's not so far to fall.'

'A wise decision, at least for the time being,' said Alec. 'Everyone should have his point of view.'

'Isn't this everyone's Point of View?' asked Tock, looking round curiously.

'Of course not,' replied Alec, sitting himself down on nothing. 'It's only mine, and you certainly can't always look at things from someone else's point of view. For instance, from here that looks like a bucket of water,' he said, pointing to a bucket of water; 'but from an ant's point of view it's a vast ocean, from an elephant's just a cool drink, and to a fish, of course, it's home. So, you see, the way you see things depends a great deal on where you look at them from. Now, come along and I'll show you the rest of the forest.'

He ran quickly through the air, stopping occasionally to beckon Milo, Tock, and the Humbug along, and they followed as well as anyone who had to stay on the ground could.

'Does everyone here grow the way you do?' puffed Milo when he had caught up.

'Almost everyone,' replied Alec, and then he stopped a moment and thought. 'Now and then, though, someone does begin to grow differently. Instead of down, his feet grow up towards the sky. But we do our best to discourage awkward things like that.'

'What happens to *them*?' insisted Milo.

'Oddly enough, they often grow ten times the size of everyone else,' said Alec thoughtfully, 'and I've heard that they walk among the stars.' And with that he skipped off once again towards the waiting woods.

# 10      *A Colourful Symphony*

As they ran, tall trees closed in around them and arched gracefully towards the sky. The late-afternoon sunlight leaped lightly from leaf to leaf, slid along branches and down trunks, and dropped finally to the ground in warm, luminous patches. A soft glow filled the air with the kind of light that made everything look sharp and clear and close enough to reach out and touch.

Alec raced ahead, laughing and shouting, but soon encountered serious difficulties; for, while he could always see the tree behind the next one, he could never see the next one itself and was continually crashing into it. After several minutes of wildly dashing about, they all stopped for a breath of air.

'I think we're lost,' panted the Humbug, collapsing into a large bramble bush.

'Nonsense!' shouted Alec from the high branch on which he sat.

'Do you know where we are?' asked Milo.

'Certainly,' he replied, 'we're right here on this very spot. Besides, being lost is never a matter of not knowing where you are; it's a matter of not knowing where you aren't – and I don't care at all about where I'm not.'

This was much too complicated for the bug to work out,

and Milo had just begun repeating it to himself when Alec said, 'If you don't believe me, ask the giant,' and he pointed to a small house tucked neatly between two of the largest trees.

Milo and Tock walked up to the door, whose brass name-plate read simply THE GIANT, and knocked.

'Good afternoon,' said the perfectly ordinary-sized man who answered the door.

'Are you the giant?' asked Tock doubtfully.

'To be sure,' he replied proudly. 'I'm the smallest giant in the world. What can I do for you?'

'Are we lost?' said Milo.

'That's a difficult question,' said the giant. 'Why don't you go round to the back and ask the midget?' And he closed the door.

They walked to the rear of the house, which looked exactly like the front, and knocked at the door, whose name-plate read THE MIDGET.

'How are you?' inquired the man, who looked exactly like the giant.

'Are you the midget?' asked Tock, again with a hint of uncertainty in his voice.

'Unquestionably,' he answered. 'I'm the tallest midget in the world. May I help you?'

'Do you think we're lost?' repeated Milo.

'That's a very complicated problem,' he said. 'Why don't you go round to the side and ask the fat man?' And he, too, quickly disappeared.

The side of the house looked very like the front and back, and the door flew open the very instant they knocked.

'How nice of you to come by,' exclaimed the man, who could have been the midget's twin brother.

'You must be the fat man,' said Tock, learning not to count too much on appearance.

'The thinnest one in the world,' he replied brightly: 'but

95

if you have any questions, I suggest you try the thin man, on the other side of the house.'

Just as they suspected, the other side of the house looked the same as the front, the back, and the side, and the door was again answered by a man who looked precisely like the other three.

'What a pleasant surprise!' he cried happily. 'I haven't had a visitor for as long as I can remember.'

'How long is that?' asked Milo.

'I'm sure I don't know,' he replied. 'Now pardon me; I have to answer the door.'

'But you just did,' said Tock.

'Oh yes, I'd forgotten.'

'Are you the fattest thin man in the world?' asked Tock.

'Do you know one that's fatter?' he asked impatiently.

'I think you're all the same man,' said Milo emphatically.

'S-S-S-S-S-H-H-H-H-H-H-H,' he cautioned, putting his finger up to his lips and drawing Milo closer. 'Do you want to ruin everything? You see, to tall men I'm a midget, and to short

men I'm a giant; to the skinny ones I'm a fat man, and to the
fat ones I'm a thin man. That way I can hold four jobs at once.
As you can see, though, I'm neither tall nor short nor fat nor
thin. In fact, I'm quite ordinary, but there are so many
ordinary men that no one asks their opinion about anything.
Now what is your question?'

'Are we lost?' asked Milo once again.

'H-h-m-m-m,' said the man, scratching his head. 'I haven't
had such a difficult question for as long as I can remember.
Would you mind repeating it? It's slipped my mind.'

Milo asked the question for the fifth time.

'My, my,' the man mumbled. 'I know one thing for certain;
it's much harder to tell whether you *are* lost than whether you
*were* lost, for, on many occasions, where you're going is
exactly where you are. On the other hand, you often find that
where you've been is not at all where you should have gone,
and, since it's much more difficult to find your way back from
somewhere you've never left, I suggest you go there immediately and then decide. If you have any more questions, please

**D**

ask the giant.' And he slammed his door and pulled down the blind.

'I hope you're satisfied,' said Alec when they'd returned from the house, and he bounced to his feet, bent down to wake up the snoring Humbug, and started off, more slowly this time, in the direction of a large clearing.

'Do many people live here in the forest?' asked Milo as they trotted along together.

'Oh yes, they live in a wonderful city called Reality,' he announced, smashing into one of the smaller trees and sending a cascade of nuts and leaves to the ground. 'It's just along here.'

In a few more steps the forest opened before them, and off to the left a magnificent metropolis appeared. The roof-tops shone like mirrors, the walls glistened with thousands of precious stones, and the broad avenues were paved in silver.

'Is that it?' shouted Milo, running towards the shining streets.

'Oh no, that's only Illusions,' said Alec. 'The real city is over there.'

98

'What are Illusions?' Milo asked, for it was the loveliest city he'd ever seen.

'Illusions,' explained Alec, 'are like mirages,' and, realizing that this didn't help much, he continued: 'And mirages are things that aren't really there that you can see very clearly.'

'How can you see something that isn't there?' yawned the Humbug, who wasn't fully awake yet.

'Sometimes it's much simpler than seeing things that are,' he said. 'For instance, if something is there, you can only see it with your eyes open, but if it isn't there, you can see it just as well with your eyes closed. That's why imaginary things are often easier to see than real ones.'

'Then where is Reality?' barked Tock.

'Here,' cried Alec, waving his arms. 'You're standing in the middle of the High Street.'

They looked around very carefully. Tock sniffed suspiciously at the wind and the Humbug gingerly stabbed his cane at the air, but there was nothing at all to see.

'It's really a very pleasant city,' said Alec as he strolled down the street, pointing out several of the sights, which didn't seem to be there, and tipping his cap to the passers-by. There were great crowds of people rushing along with their heads down, and they all appeared to know exactly where they were going as they darted down and around the non-existent streets and in and out of the missing buildings.

'I don't see any city,' said Milo softly.

'Neither do they,' Alec remarked sadly, 'but it hardly matters, for they don't miss it at all.'

'It must be very difficult to live in a city you can't see,' Milo insisted, jumping aside as a line of cars and vans went by.

'Not at all, once you get used to it,' said Alec. 'But let me tell you how it happened.' And, as they strolled along the bustling busy street, he began.

'Many years ago, on this very spot, there was a beautiful city of fine houses and inviting spaces, and no one who lived here was ever in a hurry. The streets were full of wonderful

things to see and the people would often stop to look at them.'

'Didn't they have anywhere to go?' asked Milo.

'To be sure,' continued Alec; 'but, as you know, the most important reason for going from one place to another is to see what's in between, and they took great pleasure in doing just that. Then one day someone discovered that if you walked as fast as possible and looked at nothing but your shoes you would arrive at your destination much more quickly. Soon everyone was doing it. They all rushed down the avenues and hurried along the boulevards seeing nothing of the wonders and beauties of their city as they went.'

Milo remembered the many times he'd done the very same thing; and, as hard as he tried, there were even things on his own street that he couldn't remember.

'No one paid any attention to how things looked, and as they moved faster and faster everything grew uglier and dirtier, and as everything grew uglier and dirtier they moved faster and faster, and at last a very strange thing began to happen. Because nobody cared, the city slowly began to disappear. Day by day the buildings grew fainter and fainter, and the streets faded away, until at last it was entirely invisible. There was nothing to see at all.'

'What did they do?' the Humbug inquired, suddenly taking an interest in things.

'Nothing at all,' continued Alec. 'They went on living here just as they'd always done, in the houses they could no longer see and on the streets which had vanished, because nobody had noticed a thing. And that's the way they have lived to this very day.'

'Hasn't anyone told them?' asked Milo.

'It doesn't do any good,' Alec replied, 'for they can never see what they're in too much of a hurry to look for.'

'Why don't they live in Illusions?' suggested the Humbug. 'It's much prettier.'

'Many of them do,' he answered, walking in the direction of the forest once again, 'but it's just as bad to live in a place where what you do see isn't there as it is to live in one where what you don't see is.'

'Perhaps some day you can have one city as easy to see as Illusions and as hard to forget as Reality,' Milo remarked.

'That will happen only when you bring back Rhyme and Reason,' said Alec, smiling, for he had seen right through Milo's plans. 'Now let's hurry or we'll miss the evening concert.'

They followed him quickly up a flight of steps which couldn't be seen and through a door which didn't exist. In a moment they had left Reality (which is sometimes a hard thing to tell) and stood in a completely different part of the forest.

The sun was dropping slowly from sight, and stripes of purple and orange and crimson and gold piled themselves on top of the distant hills. The last shafts of light waited patiently for a flight of wrens to find their way home, and a group of anxious stars had already taken their places.

'Here we are!' cried Alec, and, with a sweep of his arm, he pointed towards an enormous symphony orchestra. 'Isn't it a grand sight?'

There were at least a thousand musicians ranged in a great arc before them. To the left and right were the violins and 'cellos, whose bows moved in great waves, and behind them in numberless profusion the piccolos, flutes, clarinets, oboes, bassoons, horns, trumpets, trombones and tubas were all playing at once. At the very rear, so far away that they could hardly be seen, were the percussion instruments, and lastly, in a long line up one side of a steep slope, were the solemn bass fiddles.

On a high podium in front stood the conductor, a tall, gaunt man with dark deep-set eyes and a thin mouth placed carelessly between his long pointed nose and his long pointed chin. He used no baton, but conducted with large, sweeping movements which seemed to start at his toes and work slowly

up through his body and along his slender arms and end finally at the tips of his graceful fingers.

'I don't hear any music,' said Milo.

'That's right,' said Alec; 'you don't listen to this concert – you watch it. Now, pay attention.'

As the conductor waved his arms, he moulded the air like handfuls of soft clay, and the musicians carefully followed his every direction.

'What are they playing?' asked Tock, looking up inquisitively at Alec.

'The sunset, of course. They play it every evening, about this time.'

'They do?' said Milo quizzically.

'Naturally,' answered Alec; 'and they also play morning, noon, and night, when, of course, it's morning, noon, or night. Why, there wouldn't be any colour in the world unless they played it. Each instrument plays a different one,' he explained, 'and depending, of course, on what season it is and how the weather's to be, the conductor chooses his score and directs the day. But watch: the sun has almost set, and in a moment you can ask Chroma himself.'

The last colours slowly faded from the western sky, and, as they did, one by one the instruments stopped, until only the bass fiddles, in their sombre slow movement, were left to play the night and a single set of silver bells brightened the constellations. The conductor let his arms fall limply at his sides and stood quite still as darkness claimed the forest.

'That was a very beautiful sunset,' said Milo, walking to the podium.

'It should be,' was the reply: 'we've been practising since the world began.' And, reaching down, the speaker picked Milo off the ground and set him on the music stand. 'I am Chroma the Great,' he continued, gesturing broadly with his hands, 'conductor of colour, maestro of pigment, and director of the entire spectrum.'

'Do you play all day long?' asked Milo when he had introduced himself.

'Ah yes, all day, every day,' he sang out, then pirouetted gracefully around the platform. 'I rest only at night, and even then *they* play on.'

'But what would happen if you stopped?' asked Milo, who didn't quite believe that colour happened like that.

'See for yourself,' roared Chroma, and he raised both hands high over his head. Immediately the instruments that were playing stopped, and at once all colour vanished. The world looked like an enormous colouring book that had never been used. Everything appeared in simple black outlines, and it looked as if someone with a set of paints the size of a house and a brush as wide could stay happily occupied for years. Then Chroma lowered his arms. The instruments began again and the colour returned.

'You see what a dull place the world would be without colour?' he said, bowing until his chin almost touched the ground. 'But what pleasure to lead my violins in a serenade of spring green or hear my trumpets blare out the blue sea and then watch the oboes tint it all in warm yellow sunshine. And rainbows are best of all – and blazing neon signs, and taxicabs with stripes, and the soft, muted tones of a foggy day. We play them all.'

While Chroma was speaking, Milo sat with his eyes open wide, and Alec, Tock, and the Humbug looked on in wonder.

'Now I really must get some sleep,' Chroma yawned. 'We've had lightning, fireworks, and parades for the last few nights, and I've had to be up to conduct them. But tonight is sure to be quiet.' Then, putting his large hand on Milo's shoulder, he said, 'Be a good fellow and watch my orchestra till morning, will you? And be sure to wake me at 5.23 for sunrise. Good night, good night, good night.'

With that he leaped lightly from the podium and, in three long steps, vanished into the forest.

'That's a good idea,' said Tock, making himself comfortable in the grass as the bug grumbled himself quickly to sleep and Alec stretched out in mid-air.

And Milo, full of thoughts and questions, curled up on the pages of tomorrow's music and eagerly awaited the dawn.

## 11 *Dischord and Dynne*

One by one, the hours passed, and at exactly 5.22 (by Tock's very accurate clock) Milo carefully opened one eye and, in a moment, the other. Everything was still purple, dark blue, and black, yet scarcely a minute remained to the long, quiet night.

He stretched lazily, rubbed his eyelids, scratched his head, and shivered once as a greeting to the early-morning mist.

'I must wake Chroma for the sunrise,' he said softly. Then he suddenly wondered what it would be like to lead the orchestra and to colour the whole world himself.

The idea whirled through his thoughts until he quickly decided that since it couldn't be very difficult, and since they probably all knew what to do by themselves anyway, and since it did seem a shame to wake anyone so early, and since it might be his only chance to try, and since the musicians were already poised and ready, he would – but just for a little while.

And so, as everyone slept peacefully on, Milo stood on tip-toes, raised his arms slowly in front of him, and made the slightest movement possible with the index finger of his right hand. It was now 5.23 a.m.

As if understanding his signal perfectly, a single piccolo played a single note and off in the east a solitary shaft of cool lemon light flicked across the sky. Milo smiled happily and

then cautiously crooked his finger again. This time two more piccolos and a flute joined in and three more rays of light danced lightly into view. Then with both hands he made a great circular sweep in the air and watched with delight as all the musicians began to play at once.

The 'cellos made the hills glow red, and the leaves and grass were tipped with a soft pale green as the violins began their song. Only the bass fiddles rested as the entire orchestra washed the forest in colour.

Milo was overjoyed because they were all playing for him, and just the way they should.

'Won't Chroma be surprised?' he thought, signalling the musicians to stop. 'I'll wake him now.'

But, instead of stopping, they continued to play even louder than before, until each colour became more brilliant than he thought possible. Milo shielded his eyes with one hand and waved the other desperately, but the colours continued to grow brighter and brighter and brighter, until an even more curious thing began to happen.

As Milo frantically conducted, the sky changed slowly from blue to tan and then to a rich magenta red. Flurries of light-green snow began to fall, and the leaves on the trees and bushes turned a vivid orange.

All the flowers suddenly appeared black, the grey rocks became a lovely soft chartreuse, and even peacefully sleeping Tock changed from brown to a magnificent ultramarine. Nothing was the colour it should have been, and yet, the more he tried to straighten things out, the worse they became.

'I wish I hadn't started,' he thought unhappily as a pale-blue blackbird flew by. 'There doesn't seem to be any way to stop them.'

He tried very had to do everything just the way Chroma

had done, but nothing worked. The musicians played on, faster and faster, and the purple sun raced quickly across the sky. In less than a minute it had set once more in the west and then, without any pause, risen again in the east. The sky was now quite yellow and the grass a charming shade of lavender. Seven times the sun rose and almost as quickly disappeared as the colours kept changing. In just a few minutes a whole week had gone by.

At last the exhausted Milo, afraid to call for help and on the verge of tears, dropped his hands to his sides. The orchestra stopped. The colours disappeared, and once again it was night. The time was 5.27 a.m.

'Wake up, everybody! Time for the sunrise!' he shouted with relief, and quickly jumped from the music stand.

'What a marvellous rest,' said Chroma, striding to the podium. 'I feel as though I'd slept for a week. My, my, I see we're a little late this morning. I'll have to cut my lunch hour short by four minutes.'

He tapped for attention, and this time the dawn proceeded perfectly.

'You did a fine job,' he said, patting Milo on the head. 'Some day I'll let you conduct the orchestra yourself.'

Tock wagged his tail proudly, but Milo didn't say a word, and to this day no one knows of the lost week but the few people who happened to be awake at 5.23 on that very strange morning.

'We'd better be getting along,' said Tock, whose alarm had begun to ring again, 'for there's still a long way to go.'

Chroma nodded a fond good-bye as they all started back through the forest, and in honour of the visit he made all the wild flowers bloom in a breath-taking display.

'I'm sorry you can't stay longer,' said Alec sadly. 'There's so much more to see in the Forest of Sight. But I suppose there's a lot to see everywhere, if only you keep your eyes open.'

They walked for a while, all silent in their thoughts until they reached the car and Alec drew a fine telescope from his shirt and handed it to Milo.

'Carry this with you on your journey,' he said softly, 'for there is much worth noticing that often escapes the eye. Through it you can see everything from the tender moss in a pavement crack to the glow of the farthest star – and, most important of all, you can see things as they really are, not just as they seem to be. It's my gift to you.'

Milo placed the telescope carefully in the glove compartment, and reached up to shake Alec by the hand. Then he stepped on the starter and, with his head full of strange new thoughts, drove out at the far end of the forest.

The easy rolling countryside now stretched before them in a series of dips and rises that leaped up one side of each crest and slid gently down the other in a way that made stomachs laugh and faces frown. As they topped the brow of the highest hill, a deep valley appeared ahead. The road, finally making up its mind, plummeted down, as if anxious to renew acquaintance with the sparkling blue stream that flowed below. When they reached the floor of the valley the wind grew stronger as it funnelled through the rocks, and directly ahead a bright-coloured speck grew larger and larger.

'It looks like a wagon,' cried Milo excitedly.

'It *is* a wagon – a carnival wagon,' seconded Tock. And that's exactly what it was – parked at the side of the road, painted bright red, and looking quite deserted. On its side in enormous white letters bordered in black was the inscription KAKOFONOUS A. DISCHORD, and below in slightly smaller black letters bordered in white was DOCTOR OF DISSONANCE.

'Perhaps if someone's at home he might tell us how far we have to go,' said Milo, parking next to the wagon.

He tiptoed timidly up the three wooden steps to the door, tapped lightly, and leaped back in fright, for the moment he

knocked there was a terrific crash from inside the wagon that
sounded as if a whole set of dishes had been dropped from the
ceiling on to a hard stone floor. At the same time the door
flew open, and from the dark interior a hoarse voice inquired,
'Have you ever heard a whole set of dishes dropped from the
ceiling on to a hard stone floor?'

Milo, who had tumbled back off the steps, sat up quickly,
while Tock and the Humbug rushed from the car to see what
had happened.

'Well, have you?' insisted the voice, which was so raspy
that it made you want to clear your own throat.

'Not until just now,' replied Milo, getting to his feet.

'Ha! I thought not,' said the voice happily. 'Have you ever
heard an ant wearing fur slippers walk across a thick wool
carpet?' And, before they could answer, he went on in his
strange croaking way: 'Well, don't just stand there in the
cold; come in, come in. It's lucky you happened to pass; none
of you looks well.'

The faint glow of a ceiling lamp dimly illuminated the
wagon as they cautiously stepped inside – Tock first, eager to
defend against all dangers; Milo next, frightened but curious;
and the Humbug last, ready at any moment to run for his
life.

'That's right; now let's have a look at you,' he said.
'T-T-T-T-T. Very bad, very bad; a serious case.'

The dusty wagon was lined with shelves full of curious
boxes and jars of a kind found in old apothecary shops. It
looked as though it hadn't been swept out for years. Bits and
pieces of equipment lay strewn all over the floor, and at the
rear was a heavy wooden table covered with books, bottles,
and bric-à-brac.

'Have you ever heard a blindfolded octopus unwrap a
Cellophane-covered bathtub?' he inquired again as the air
was filled with a loud, crinkling, snapping sound.

Sitting at the table, busily mixing and measuring, was the

man who had invited them in. He was wearing a long white coat with a stethoscope around his neck and a small round mirror attached to his forehead, and the only really noticeable things about him were his tiny moustache and his enormous ears, each of which was fully as large as his head.

'Are you a doctor?' asked Milo, trying to feel as well as possible.

'I am KAKOFONOUS A. DISCHORD, DOCTOR OF DISSONANCE,' roared the man, and, as he spoke, several small explosions and a grinding crash were heard.

'What does the 'A' stand for?' stammered the nervous bug, too frightened to move.

'AS LOUD AS POSSIBLE,' bellowed the doctor, and two screeches and a bump accompanied his response. 'Now, step a little closer and stick out your tongues.

'Just as I suspected,' he continued, opening a large dusty book and thumbing back the pages. 'You're suffering from a severe lack of noise.'

He began to jump around the wagon, snatching bottles from the shelves until he had a large assortment in various colours and sizes collected at one end of the table. All were neatly labelled: Loud Cries, Soft Cries, Bangs, Bongs, Smashes, Crashes, Swishes, Swooshes, Snaps, and Crackles, Whistles and Gongs, Squeaks, Squawks, and Miscellaneous Uproar. After pouring a little of each into a large glass beaker, he stirred the mixture thoroughly with a wooden spoon, watching intently as it smoked and steamed and boiled and bubbled.

'Be ready in just a moment,' he explained, rubbing his hands.

Milo had never seen such unpleasant-looking medicine and wasn't at all anxious to try any. 'Just what kind of a doctor are you?' he asked suspiciously.

'Well, you might say I'm a specialist,' said the doctor. 'I specialize in noise – all kinds – from the loudest to the softest,

and from the slightly annoying to the terribly unpleasant. For instance, have you ever heard a square-wheeled steam roller ride over a street full of hard-boiled eggs?' he asked, and, as he did, all that could be heard were loud crunching sounds.

'But who would want all those terrible noises?' asked Milo, holding his ears.

'Everybody does,' said the surprised doctor; 'they're very popular today. Why, I'm kept so busy I can hardly fill the orders for noise pills, racket lotion, clamour salve, and hubbub tonic. That's all people seem to want these days.'

He stirred the beaker of liquid a few more times and then, as the steam cleared, continued:

'Business wasn't always so good. Years ago, everyone wanted pleasant sounds and, except for a few orders during wars and earthquakes, things were very bad. But then the big cities were built and there was a great need for honking horns, screeching trains, clanging bells, deafening shouts, piercing shrieks, gurgling drains and all the rest of those wonderfully unpleasant sounds we use so much of today. Without them people would be very unhappy, so I make sure that they get as much as they want. Why, if you take a little of my medicine every day, you'll never have to hear a beautiful sound again. Here, try some.'

'If it's all the same to you, I'd rather not,' said the Humbug, backing away into the far corner of the wagon.

'I don't want to be cured of beautiful sounds,' insisted Milo.

'Besides,' growled Tock, who decided that he didn't much like Dr Dischord, 'there is no such illness as lack of noise.'

'Of course not,' replied the doctor, pouring himself a small glass of the liquid; 'that's what makes it so difficult to cure. I only treat illnesses that don't exist: that way, if I can't cure them, there's no harm done – just one of the precautions of the trade,' he concluded, and, seeing that no one was about to take his medicine, he again reached towards the shelf, removed a dark-amber bottle, dusted it carefully, and placed it on the table in front of him.

'Very well, if you want to go all through life suffering from a noise deficiency, I'll give it all to the D Y N N E for his lunch,' he said, and he uncorked the bottle with a hollow-sounding pop.

For a moment everything was quiet as Milo, Tock, and the Humbug looked intently at the bottle, wondering what Dr Dischord would do next. Then, very faintly at first, they heard a low rumbling that sounded miles away. It grew louder and louder and louder and closer and closer and closer until it became a deafening, ear-splitting roar that seemed to be coming from inside the tiny bottle. Then, from the bottle, a thick bluish smog spiralled to the ceiling, spread out, and gradually assumed the shape of a thick bluish smog with hands, feet, bright-yellow eyes, and a large frowning mouth. As soon as the smog was completely out of the bottle it grasped the beaker of liquid, tilted back what would have been its head, if it really had one, and drank it all in three gulps

'A-H-H-H, THAT WAS GOOD, MASTER,' he bellowed, shaking the whole wagon. 'I thought you'd never let me out. Terribly cramped in there.'

'This is my assistant, the awful DYNNE,' said Dr Dischord. 'You must forgive his appearance, for he really doesn't have any. You see, he is an orphan whom I raised myself without benefit of governess or any other assistance for –'

'No nurse is good nurse,' interrupted the DYNNE doubling up with laughter (if you can imagine a thick bluish smog doubling up with laughter).

'For I found him,' continued the doctor, ignoring this outburst, 'living alone and unwanted in an abandoned soda bottle – without family or relatives –'

'No niece is good niece,' roared the DYNNE again, with a laugh that sounded like several sirens going off at once, and he slapped at where his knee should have been.

'And brought him here,' continued the exasperated Dischord, 'where, despite his lack of shape or features, I trained –'

'No nose is good nose,' thundered the DYNNE once again as he collapsed in another fit of hysterics and clutched his sides.

'I trained him as my assistant in the business of concocting and dispensing noise,' finished the doctor, mopping his brow with a handkershief.

'No noise is good noise,' exclaimed the Humbug happily, trying to catch the spirit of things.

'THAT'S NOT FUNNY AT ALL,' sobbed the DYNNE, who went to a corner and sulked.

'What is a DYNNE?' asked Milo when he had recovered from the shock of seeing him appear.

'You mean you've never met the awful DYNNE before?' said Dr Dischord in a surprised tone. 'Why, I thought everyone had. When you're playing in your room and making a great amount of noise, what do they tell you to stop?'

'That awful din,' admitted Milo.

'When the neighbours are playing their radio too loud, late at night, what do you wish they'd turn down?'

'The awful din,' answered Tock.

'When the street where you live is being repaired and the pneumatic drills are working all day, what does everyone complain of?'

'The dreadful row,' volunteered the Humbug brightly.

'The dreadful RAUW,' cried the anguished DYNNE, 'was my grandfather. He perished in the great silence epidemic of 1712.'

Milo felt so sorry for the unhappy DYNNE that he gave him his handkerchief, which was immediately covered in bluish smoggy tears.

'Thank you,' groaned the DYNNE; 'that's very kind. But I certainly can't understand why you don't like noise,' he said. 'Why, I heard an explosion last week that was so lovely I cried for two days.'

The very thought of it upset him so much that he began to sob all over again in a way that sounded almost exactly like a handful of fingernails being scratched across a mile-long blackboard. He buried his head in the doctor's lap.

'He's very sensitive, isn't he?' asked Milo, trying to comfort the emotional DYNNE.

'It's true,' agreed Dr Dischord. 'But he's right, you know, for noise is the most valuable thing in the world.'

'King Azaz says words are,' said Milo.

'NONSENSE,' the doctor roared. 'Why, when a baby wants food, how does he ask?'

'He screams!' answered the DYNNE, looking up happily.

'And when an automobile wants petrol?'

'It chokes!' he shouted again, jumping for joy.

'When a river wants water, what does it do?'

'It creaks!' bellowed the DYNNE as he collapsed into a fit of uncontrolled laughter.

'And what happens when a new day begins?'

'It breaks!' he gasped joyfully from the floor, a look of utter bliss covering his face.

'You see how simple it is,' the doctor said to Milo, who didn't see at all. And then, turning to the tear-stained, smiling DYNNE, he remarked, 'Isn't it time for you to go?'

'Where to?' asked Milo. 'Perhaps we're going the same way.'

'I think not,' the DYNNE replied, picking up an armful of empty sacks from the table, 'for I'm going on my noise collection rounds. You see, once a day I travel throughout the kingdom and collect all the wonderfully horrible and beautifully unpleasant noises that have been made, pack them into my sacks, and bring them back here for the doctor to make his medicines from.'

'And a good job he does,' said Dr Dischord, pounding his fist on the table.

'So, wherever the noise is, that's where you'll find me,' said the DYNNE with an appreciative smile; 'and I must hurry along, for I understand that today there's to be a screech, several loud crashes, and a bit of pandemonium.'

'And in which direction are you going?' asked the doctor, mixing another brew.

'To Digitopolis,' replied Milo.

'How unfortunate,' he said as the DYNNE shuffled towards the door; 'how very unfortunate, for then you must pass through the Valley of Sound.'

'Is that bad?' asked the perpetually worried Humbug.

The DYNNE paused in the doorway with a look of extreme

horror on his almost featureless face, and the doctor shuddered in a way that sounded very much like a fast-moving freight train being derailed into a mountain of custard.

'Well you might ask, for you will find out soon enough,' was all he would say as he sadly bade them farewell and the DYNNE galloped off on his rounds.

## 12 *The Silent Valley*

'How agreeable and pleasant this valley is,' thought Milo as once again they bounced along the highway, with the Humbug humming snatches of old songs, to his own vast amusement, and Tock sniffing contentedly at the wind.

'I really can't see what Dr Dischord was so concerned about; there certainly couldn't be anything unpleasant along this road.' And just as the thought crossed his mind they passed through a heavy stone gateway and everything was very different.

At first it was difficult to tell just what had changed – it all looked the same and it all smelled the same – but, for some reason, nothing sounded the same.

'I wonder what's happened?' said Milo. At least that's what he tried to say, for, although his lips moved, not a sound came from his mouth.

And suddenly he realized what it was, for Tock was no no longer ticking and the Humbug, although happily singing, was doing so in complete silence. The wind no longer rustled the leaves, the car no longer squeaked, and the insects no longer buzzed in the fields. Not the slightest thing could be heard, and it felt as if, in some mysterious way, a switch had been thrown and all the sound in the world had been turned off at the same instant.

The Humbug, suddenly realizing what had happened, leaped to his feet in terror, and Tock worriedly checked to see if he was still keeping time. It was certainly a strange feeling to know that no matter how loudly or softly you chatted or rattled or bumped, it all came out the same way – as nothing.

'How dreadful,' thought Milo as he slowed down the car.

The three of them began to talk and shout at once with absolutely no result until, hardly noticing where they were going, they had driven into the midst of a large crowd of people marching along the road. Some of them were singing at the tops of their non-existent voices and the others were carrying large signs which proclaimed:

DOWN WITH SILENCE

ALL QUIET IS NO DIET

IT'S LAUDABLE TO BE AUDIBLE

MORE SOUND FOR ALL

And one enormous banner stated simply:

HEAR HERE

Except for these, and the big brass cannon being pulled along behind, they all looked very much like the residents of any other small valley to which you've never been.

When the car had stopped, one of them held up a placard which said: WELCOME TO THE VALLEY OF SOUND. And the others cheered as loudly as possible, which was not very loud at all.

'HAVE YOU COME TO HELP US?' asked another, stepping forward with his question.

'PLEASE!' added a third.

Milo tried desperately to say who he was and where he was going, but to no avail. As he did, four more placards announced:

LOOK CAREFULLY

AND WE

WILL TELL YOU

OF OUR TERRIBLE MISFORTUNE

And while two of them held up a large blackboard, a third, writing as fast as he could, explained why there was nothing but quiet in the Valley of Sound.

'At a place in the valley not far from here,' he began, 'where the echoes used to gather and the winds came to rest, there is a great stone fortress, and in it lives the Sound-keeper, who rules this land. When the old king of Wisdom drove the demons into the distant mountains, he appointed her guardian of all sounds and noises, past, present, and future.

'For years she ruled as a wise and beloved monarch, each morning at sunrise releasing the day's new sounds, to be borne by the winds throughout the kingdom, and each night at moonset gathering in the old sounds, to be catalogued and filed in the vast storage vaults below.'

The writer paused for a moment to mop his brow and then,

since the blackboard was full, erased it completely and continued anew from the top.

'She was generous to a fault and provided us with all the sound we could possibly use: for singing as we worked, for bubbling pots of stew, for the chop of an axe and the crash of a tree, for the creak of a hinge and the hoot of an owl, for the squish of a shoe in the mud and the friendly tapping of rain on the roof, and for the sweet music of pipes and the sharp snap of winter ice cracking on the ground.'

He paused again as a tear of longing rolled from cheek to lip with the sweet-salty taste of an old memory.

'And all these sounds, when once used, would be carefully placed in alphabetical order and neatly kept for future reference. Everyone lived in peace, and the valley flourished as the happy home of sound. But then things began to change.

'Slowly at first, and then in a rush, more people came to settle here and brought with them new ways and new sounds, some very beautiful and some less so. But everyone was so busy with the things that had to be done that they scarcely had time to listen at all. And, as you know, a sound which is not heard disappears for ever and is not to be found again.

'People laughed less and grumbled more, sang less and shouted more, and the sounds they made grew louder and uglier. It became difficult to hear even the birds or the breeze, and soon everyone stopped listening for them.'

He again cleared the blackboard, as the Humbug choked back a sob, and continued writing.

'The Soundkeeper grew worried and disconsolate. Each day there were fewer sounds to be collected, and most of those were hardly worth keeping. Many people thought it was the weather, and others blamed the moon, but the general consensus of opinion held that the trouble began at the time that Rhyme and Reason were banished. But, no matter what the cause, no one knew what to do.

'Then one day Dr Dischord appeared in the valley with his

wagon of medicines and the bluish smoggy DYNNE. He made a thorough examination and promised to cure everyone of everything; and the Soundkeeper let him try.

'He gave several bad-tasting spoonfuls of medicine to every adult and child, and it worked – but not really as expected. For he cured everybody of everything *but* noise. The Soundkeeper became furious. She chased him from the valley for ever and then issued the following decree:

'FROM THIS DAY FORWARD THE VALLEY OF SOUND SHALL BE SILENT. SINCE SOUND IS NO LONGER APPRECIATED, I HEREBY ABOLISH IT. PLEASE RETURN ALL UNUSED AMOUNTS TO THE FORTRESS IMMEDIATELY.

'And that's the way it has been ever since,' he concluded sadly. 'There is nothing we can do to change it, and each day new hardships are reported.'

A small man, with his arms full of letters and messages, pushed through the crowd and offered them to Milo. Milo took one which read:

Dear Soundkeeper,
We had a thunderstorm last week and the thunder still hasn't arrived. How long should we wait?

Yours truly,
A friend

Then he took a telegram which stated:

BAND CONCERT GREAT SUCCESS STOP WHEN MAY WE EXPECT THE MUSIC STOP

'Now you see,' continued the writer, 'why you must help us attack the fortress and free sound.'

'What can I do?' wrote Milo.

'You must visit the Soundkeeper and bring from the fortress one sound, no matter how small, with which to load our cannon. For, if we reach the walls with the slightest noise,

they will collapse and free the rest. It won't be easy, for she is hard to deceive, but you must try.'

Milo thought for just a moment and then, with a resolute 'I shall,' volunteered to go.

Within a few minutes he stood bravely at the fortress door. 'Knock, knock,' he wrote neatly on a piece of paper, which he pushed under the crack. In a moment the great portal swung open, and as it closed behind him, a gentle voice sang out:

'Right this way; I'm in the parlour.'

'Can I talk now?' cried Milo happily, hearing his voice once again.

'Yes, but only in here,' she replied softly. 'Now do come into the parlour.'

Milo walked slowly down the long hall and into the little room where the Soundkeeper sat listening intently to an enormous radio set, whose switches, dials, knobs, meters, and speaker covered one whole wall, and which at the moment was playing nothing.

'Isn't that lovely?' she sighed. 'It's my favourite programme – fifteen minutes of silence – and after that there's a half-hour of quiet and then an interlude of lull. Why, did you know that there are almost as many kinds of stillness as there are sounds? But, sadly enough, no one pays any attention to them these days.

'Have you ever heard the wonderful silence just before the dawn?' she inquired. 'Or the quiet and calm just as a storm ends? Or perhaps you know the silence when you haven't the answer to a question you've been asked, or the hush of a country road at night, or the expectant pause in a roomful of people when someone is just about to speak, or, most beautiful of all, the moment after the door closes and you're all alone in the whole house? Each one is different, you know, and all very beautiful, if you listen carefully.'

As she spoke, the thousands of little bells and chimes which covered her from head to toe tinkled softly and, as if in reply, the telephone began to ring, too.

'For someone who loves silence, she certainly talks a great deal,' thought Milo.

'At one time I was able to listen to any sound made in any place at any time,' the Soundkeeper remarked, pointing towards the radio wall, 'but now I merely –'

'Pardon me,' interrupted Milo as the phone continued to ring, 'but aren't you going to answer it?'

'Oh no, not in the middle of the programme,' she replied, and turned the silence up a little louder.

'But it may be important,' insisted Milo.

'Not at all,' she assured him; 'it's only me. It gets so lonely around here, with no sounds to distribute or collect, that I phone myself seven or eight times a day just to see how I am.'

'How are you?' he asked politely.

'Not very well, I'm afraid. I seem to have a touch of static,' she complained. 'But what brings you here? Of course – you've come to tour the vaults. Well, they're usually open to the public only on Mondays from two to four, but since you've travelled so far, we'll have to make an exception. Follow me, please.'

She quickly bounced to her feet with a chorus of jingles and chimes and started down the hall.

'Don't you just love jingles and chimes? I do,' she answered quickly. 'Besides, they're very convenient, for I'm always getting lost in this big fortress, and all I have to do is listen for them and then I know exactly where I am.'

They entered a tiny cagelike lift and travelled down for fully three-quarters of a minute, stopping finally in an immense vault, whose long lines of file drawers and storage bins stretched in all directions from where here began to where there ended, and from floor to ceiling.

'Every sound that's ever been made in history is kept here,' said the Soundkeeper, skipping down one of the corridors with Milo close behind. 'For instance, look here.' She opened one of the drawers and pulled out a small brown envelope. 'This is the exact tune Lord Nelson whistled as he paced the deck on that misty morning at Trafalgar in 1805.'

Milo peered into the envelope and, sure enough, that's exactly what was in it. 'But why do you collect them all?' he asked as she closed the drawer.

'If we didn't collect them,' said the Soundkeeper as they continued to stroll through the vault, 'the air would be full of old sounds and noises bouncing around and bumping into things. It would be terribly confusing, because you'd never know whether you were listening to an old one or a new one. Besides, I do like to collect things, and there are more sounds than almost anything else. Why, I have everything here from the buzz of a mosquito a million years ago to what your mother said to you this morning, and if you come back here in two days, I'll tell you what she said tomorrow. It's really very simple; let me show you. Say a word – any word.'

'Hello,' said Milo, for that was all he could think of.

'Now where do you think it went?' she asked with a smile.

'I don't know,' said Milo, shrugging his shoulders. 'I always thought that –'

'Most people do,' she hummed, peering down one of the corridors. 'Now, let me see: first we find the cabinet with today's sounds. Ah, here it is. Then we look under G for greetings, then under M for Milo, and here it is already in its envelope. So, you see, the whole system is quite automatic. It's a shame we hardly use it any more.'

'That's wonderful,' gasped Milo. 'May I have one little sound as a souvenir?'

'Certainly,' she said with pride, and then, immediately thinking better of it, added, 'not. And don't try to take one, because it's strictly against the rules.'

Milo was crestfallen. He had no idea how to steal a sound, even the smallest one, for the Soundkeeper always had at least one eye carefully focused on him.

'Now for a look at the workshops,' she cried, whisking him through another door and into a large abandoned laboratory full of old pieces of equipment, all untended and rusting.

'This is where we used to invent the sounds,' she said wistfully.

'Do they have to be invented?' asked Milo, who seemed surprised at almost everything she told him. 'I thought they just *were.*'

'No one realizes how much trouble we go through to make them,' she complained. 'Why, at one time this shop was crowded and busy from morning to night.'

'But how do you invent a sound?' Milo inquired.

'Oh, that's very easy,' she said. 'First you must decide exactly what the sound looks like, for each sound has its own exact shape and size. Then you make some of them here in the shop, and grind each one three times into an invisible powder, and throw a little of each into the air every time you need it.'

'But I've never seen a sound,' Milo insisted.

'You never see them out there,' she said, waving her arm in the general direction of everywhere, 'except every once in a while on a very cold morning when they freeze. But in here we see them all the time. Here, let me show you.'

She picked up a padded stick and struck a nearby bass drum six times. Six large woolly, fluffy cotton balls, each about two feet across, rolled silently out on to the floor.

'You see,' she said, putting some of them into a large grinder. 'Now listen.' And she took a pinch of the invisible powder and threw in into the air with a 'BOOM, BOOM, BOOM'.

'Do you know what a handclap looks like?'

Milo shook his head.

'Try it,' she commanded.

He clapped his hands once and a single sheet of clean white paper fluttered to the floor. He tried it three more times and three more sheets of paper did the very same thing. And then he applauded as fast as he could and a great cascade of papers filled the air.

'Isn't that simple? And it's the same for all sounds. If you think about it, you'll soon know what each one looks like. Take laughter, for instance,' she said, laughing brightly, and a thousand tiny brightly coloured bubbles flew into the air and popped noiselessly. 'Or speech,' she continued. 'Some of it is light and airy, some sharp and pointed, but most of it, I'm afraid, is just heavy and dull.'

'How about music?' asked Milo excitedly.

'Right over here – we weave it on our looms. Symphonies are the large beautiful carpets with all the rhythms and melodies woven in. Concertos are these tapestries, and all the other bolts of cloth are serenades, waltzes, overtures, and

rhapsodies. And we also have some of the songs that you often sing,' she cried, holding up a handful of brightly coloured handkerchiefs.

She stopped for a moment and said sadly, 'We even had one section over there that did nothing but put the sound of the ocean into sea shells. This was once such a happy place.'

'Then why don't you make sound for everyone now?' he shouted, so eagerly that the Soundkeeper leaped back in surprise.

'Don't shout so, young man! If there's one thing we need more of around here, it's less noise. Now come with me and I'll tell you all about it – and put that down immediately!' Her last remark was directed towards Milo's efforts to stuff one of the large drumbeats into his back pocket.

They returned quickly to the parlour, and when the Soundkeeper had settled herself in a chair and carefully turned the radio to a special hour of hush, Milo asked his question once again, in a somewhat lower voice.

'It doesn't make me happy to hold back the sound,' she began softly, 'for if we listen to them carefully they can sometimes tell us things far better than words.'

'But if that is so,' asked Milo – and he had no doubt that it was – 'shouldn't you release them?'

'NEVER!' she cried. 'They just use them to make horrible noises which are ugly to see and worse to hear. I leave all that to Dr Dischord and that awful, awful DYNNE.'

'But some noises are good sounds, aren't they?' he insisted.

'That may be true,' she replied stubbornly, 'but if they won't make the sounds that I like, they won't make any.'

'But –' he started to say, and it got no further than that. For while he was about to say that he didn't think that that was quite fair (a thought to which the obstinate Soundkeeper might not have taken kindly) he suddenly discovered the way he would carry his little sound from the fortress. In the instant between saying the word and before it sailed off into the air he had clamped his lips shut – and the 'but' was trapped in his mouth, all made but not spoken.

'Well, I mustn't keep you all day,' she said impatiently. 'Now turn your pockets out so that I can see that you didn't steal anything and you can be on your way.'

When he had satisfied the Soundkeeper, he nodded his farewell – for it would have been most impractical to say 'Thank you' or 'Good afternoon'– and raced out of the door.

# 13 *Unfortunate Conclusions*

With his mouth shut tight, and his feet moving as fast as thoughts could make them, Milo ran all the way back to the car. There was great excitement when he arrived, as Tock raced happily down the road to greet him. The Humbug personally accepted all congratulations from the crowd.

'Where is the sound?' someone hastily scribbled on the blackboard, and they all waited anxiously for the reply.

Milo caught his breath, picked up the chalk, and explained simply, 'It's on the tip of my tongue.'

Several people excitedly threw their hats into the air, some shouted what would have been a loud hurrah, and the rest pushed the heavy cannon into place. They aimed it directly at the thickest part of the fortress wall and packed it full of gunpowder.

Milo stood on tiptoe, leaned over into the cannon's mouth and parted his lips. The small sound dropped silently to the bottom and everything was ready. In another moment the fuse was lit and sputtering.

'I hope no one gets hurt,' thought Milo, and, before he had time to think again, an immense cloud of grey and white smoke leaped from the gun and, along with it, so softly that it was hardly heard, came the sound of –

BUT

It flew towards the wall for several seconds in a high, lazy arc and then struck ever so lightly just to the right of the big door. For an instant there was an ominous stillness, quieter and more silent than ever before, as if even the air was holding its breath.

And then, almost immediately, there was a blasting, roaring, thundering smash, followed by a crushing, shattering, bursting crash, as every stone in the fortress came toppling to the ground and the vaults burst open, spilling the sounds of history into the wind.

Every sound that had ever been uttered or made, from way back to when there were none, to way up when there were too many, came hurtling out of the debris in a way that sounded as though everyone in the world was laughing, whistling, shouting, crying, singing, whispering, humming, screaming, coughing, and sneezing, all at the same time. There were bits of old speeches floating about, as well as recited lessons, gunshots from old wars, babies' cries, motor horns, waterfalls, electric fans, galloping horses, and a great deal of everything else.

For a while there was total and deafening confusion and then, almost as quickly as they'd come, all the old sounds disappeared over the hill in search of their new freedom, and things were normal again.

The people quickly went about their busy talkative business

and, as the smoke and dust cleared, only Milo, Tock, and the Humbug noticed the Soundkeeper sitting disconsolately on a pile of rubble.

'I'm terribly sorry,' said Milo sympathetically as the three of them went to console her.

'But we had to do it,' added Tock, sniffing around the ruins.

'What a terrible mess,' observed the Humbug, with his knack for saying exactly the wrong thing.

The Soundkeeper looked around with an expression of unrelieved sadness on her unhappy face.

'It will take years to collect all those sounds again,' she sobbed, 'and even longer to put them back in proper order. But it's all my fault. For you can't improve sound by having only silence. The problem is to use each at the proper time.'

As she spoke, the familiar and unmistakable *squinch-squanch*,

*squinch-squanch* of the DYNNE's heavy footsteps could be heard plodding over the hill, and when he finally appeared he was dragging an incredibly large sack behind him.

'Can anyone use these sounds?' he puffed, mopping his forehead. 'They all came over the hill at once and none of them are awful enough for me.'

The Soundkeeper peered into the sack, and there were all the sounds which had burst from the vaults.

'How nice of you to return them!' she cried happily. 'You and the doctor must come by for an evening of beautiful music when my fortress is repaired.'

The thought of it so horrified the DYNNE that he excused himself immediately and dashed off down the road in a great panic.

'I hope I haven't offended him,' she said with some concern.

'He only likes unpleasant sounds,' volunteered Tock.

'Ah, yes,' she sighed; 'I keep forgetting that many people do. But I suppose they are necessary, for you'd never really know how pleasant one was unless you knew how unpleasant it wasn't.' She paused for a moment, then continued: 'If only Rhyme and Reason were here, I'm sure things would improve.'

'That's why we're going to rescue them,' said Milo proudly.

'What a long, hard journey that will be! You'll need some nourishment,' she cried, handing Milo a small brown package, neatly wrapped and tied with string. 'Now remember: they're not for eating, but for listening, because you'll often be hungry for sounds as well as food. Here are street noises at night, train whistles a long way off, dry leaves burning, busy department stores, crunching toast, creaking bedsprings, and, of course, all kinds of laughter. There's a little of each, and in far-off lonely places I think you'll be glad to have them.'

'I'm sure we will,' replied Milo gratefully.

'Just take this road to the sea and turn left,' she told them. 'You'll soon be in Digitopolis.'

And almost before she had finished, they had said good-bye and left the valley behind them.

The shore line was peaceful and flat, and the calm sea bumped it playfully along the sandy beach. In the distance a beautiful island covered with palm trees and flowers beckoned invitingly from the sparkling water.

'Nothing can possibly go wrong now,' cried the Humbug happily, and as soon as he'd said it he leaped from the car, as if stuck by a pin, and sailed all the way to the little island.

'And we'll have plenty of time,' answered Tock, who hadn't noticed that the bug was missing – and he, too, suddenly leaped into the air and disappeared.

'It certainly couldn't be a nicer day,' agreed Milo, who was too busy looking at the road to see that the others had gone. And in a split second he was gone also.

He landed next to Tock and the terrified Humbug on the tiny island, which now looked completely different. Instead of palms and flowers, there were only rocks and the twisted stumps of long-dead trees. It certainly didn't seem like the same place they had seen from the road.

'Pardon me,' said Milo to the first man who happened by; 'can you tell me where I am?'

'Pardon me,' replied the man; 'can you tell me *who* I am?'

The man was dressed in a shaggy tweed jacket and knickers with long woollen stockings and a cap that had a peak both front and back, and he seemed as confused as he could be.

'You must know who you are,' said Milo impatiently.

'You must know where you are,' he replied with equal annoyance.

'Oh dear, this is going to be difficult,' Milo whispered to Tock. 'I wonder if we can help him.'

They conferred for a few minutes and finally the bug looked up and said, 'Can you describe yourself?'

'Yes, indeed,' the man replied happily. 'I'm as tall as can be' – and he grew straight up until all that could be seen of him were his shoes and stockings – 'and I'm as short as can be' – and he shrank down to the size of a pebble. 'I'm as generous as can be,' he said, handing each of them a large red apple, 'and I'm as selfish as can be,' he snarled, grabbing them back again.

'I'm as strong as can be,' he roared, lifting an enormous boulder over his head, 'and I'm as weak as can be,' he gasped, staggering under the weight of his hat. 'I'm as smart as can be,' he remarked in twelve different languages, 'and I'm as stupid as can be,' he admitted, putting both feet in one shoe.

'I'm as graceful as can be,' he hummed, balancing on one toe, 'and I'm as clumsy as can be,' he cried, sticking his thumb in his eye. 'I'm as fast as can be,' he announced, running around the island twice in no time at all, 'and I'm as slow as can be,' he complained, waving good-bye to a snail. 'Is that any help to you?'

Once again they conferred in busy whispers until all three agreed.

'It's really very simple,' said the Humbug, twirling his cane.

'If everything you say is true,' added Tock.

'Then, without a doubt,' Milo concluded brightly, 'you must be Canby.'

'Of course, yes, of course,' the man shouted. 'Why didn't I think of that? I'm as happy as can be.' Then he quickly sat down, put his head in his hands, and sighed. 'But I'm also as sad as can be.'

'Now will you tell me where we are?' asked Tock as he looked around the desolate island.

'To be sure,' said Canby; 'you're on the Island of Conclusions. Make yourself at home. You're apt to be here for some time.'

'But how did we get here?' asked Milo, who was still a bit puzzled by being there at all.

'You jumped, of course,' explained Canby. 'That's the way nearly everyone get here. It's really quite simple: every time you decide something without having a good reason,

you jump to Conclusions whether you like it or not. It's such an easy trip to make that I've been here hundreds of times.'

'But this is such an unpleasant-looking place,' Milo remarked.

'Yes, that's true,' admitted Canby; 'it does look much better from a distance.'

As he spoke, at least eight or nine more people sailed on to the island from every direction possible.

'Well, I'm going to jump straight back,' announced the Humbug, who took two or three practice bends, leaped as far as he could, and landed in a heap two feet away.

'That won't do at all,' scolded Canby, helping him to his feet. 'You can never jump away from Conclusions. Getting back is not so easy. That's why we're so terribly crowded here.'

That was certainly the truth, for all along the bleak shore and clustered on the rocks for as far as anyone could see were enormous crowds of people, all sadly looking out to sea.

'Isn't there even a boat?' asked Milo, anxious to get on with his trip.

'Oh no,' replied Canby, shaking his head. 'The only way back is to swim, and that's a very long and a very hard way.'

'I don't like to get wet,' moaned the unhappy bug, and he shuddered at the thought.

'Neither do they,' said Canby sadly. 'That's what keeps them here. But I wouldn't worry too much about it, for you can swim all day in the Sea of Knowledge and still come out completely dry. Most people do. But you must excuse me now. I have to greet the new arrivals. As you know, I'm as friendly as can be.'

Over the Humbug's strenuous objections, Milo and Tock decided to swim, and, protesting loudly, the bug was dragged along with them towards the sea.

Canby hurried off to answer more questions, and the last

thing he was heard to say was 'Pardon me, can you tell me who I am?'

They swam and swam for what seemed like hours, and only Tock's firm encouragement kept Milo struggling through the icy water. At last they reached the shore, thoroughly exhausted and, except for the bug, completely soaked.

'That wasn't bad at all,' the Humbug said, straightening his tie and brushing himself off. 'I must visit there again.'

'I'm sure you will,' gasped Milo. 'But from now on I'm going to have a very good reason before I make up my mind about anything. You can lose too much time jumping to Conclusions.'

The car was just where they'd left it, and in a moment they were on their way again as the road turned away from the sea and began its long climb into the mountains. The warm sun and billowy breezes dried them as they went.

'I hope we reach Digitopolis soon,' said Milo, thinking of the breakfast they hadn't eaten. 'I wonder how far it is.'

# 14 *The Dodecahedron*
## *Leads the Way*

Up ahead, the road divided into three and, as if in reply to Milo's question, an enormous road sign, pointing in all three directions, stated clearly:

*DIGITOPOLIS*

|         |            |
| ------: | ---------- |
|       5 | Miles      |
|   1,600 | Rods       |
|   8,800 | Yards      |
|  26,400 | Feet       |
| 316,800 | Inches     |
| 633,600 | Half inches |

'Let's travel by miles,' advised the Humbug, 'it's shorter.'

'Let's travel by half inches,' suggested Milo, 'it's quicker.'

'But which road should we take?' asked Tock. 'It must make a difference.'

As they argued, a most peculiar little figure stepped nimbly from behind the sign and approached them, talking all the while. 'Yes, indeed; indeed it does; certainly; my, yes; it does make a difference; undoubtedly.'

He was constructed (for that's really the only way to describe him) of a large assortment of lines and angles connected together into one solid many-sided shape – somewhat like a cube that's had all its corners cut off and then had all its corners

cut off again. Each of the edges was neatly labelled with a small letter, and each of the angles with a large one. He wore a handsome beret on top, and peering intently from one of his several surfaces was a very serious face. Perhaps if you look at the picture you'll know what I mean.

When he reached the car, the figure doffed his cap and recited in a loud clear voice:

'My angles are many.
My sides are not few.
I'm the Dodecahedron.
Who are you?'

'What's a Dodecahedron?' inquired Milo, who was barely able to pronounce the strange word.

'See for yourself,' he said, turning around slowly. 'A Dodecahedron is a mathematical shape with twelve faces.'

Just as he said it, eleven other faces appeared, one on each surface, and each one wore a different expression.

'I usually use one at a time,' he confided, as all but the smiling one disappeared again. 'It saves wear and tear. What are you called?'

'Milo,' said Milo.

'That is an odd name,' he said, changing his smiling face for a frowning one. 'And you only have one face.'

'Is that bad?' asked Milo, making sure it was still there.

'You'll soon wear it out using it for everything,' replied the Dodecahedron. 'Now I have one for smiling, one for laughing, one for crying, one for frowning, one for thinking, one for pouting, and six more besides. Is everyone with one face called a Milo?'

'Oh no,' Milo replied; 'some are called Henry or George or Robert or John or lots of other things.'

'How terribly confusing,' he cried. 'Everything here is called exactly what it is. The triangles are called triangles, the circles are called circles, and even the same numbers have the same name. Why, can you imagine what would happen if we named all the twos Henry or George or Robert or John or lots of other things? You'd have to say Robert plus John equals four, and if the four's name were Albert, things would be hopeless.'

'I never thought of it that way,' Milo admitted.

'Then I suggest you begin at once,' admonished the Dodecahedron from his admonishing face, 'for here in Digitopolis everything is quite precise.'

'Then perhaps you can help us decide which road to take,' said Milo.

'By all means,' he replied happily. 'There's nothing to it. If a small car carrying three people at thirty miles an hour for ten minutes along a road five miles long at 11.35 in the morning starts at the same time as three people who have been travelling in a little automobile at twenty miles an hour for fifteen minutes on another road exactly twice as long as one half the distance of the other, while a dog, a bug, and a boy travel an equal distance in the same time or the same distance in an equal time along a third road in mid-October, then which one arrives first and which is the best way to go?'

'Seventeen!' shouted the Humbug, scribbling furiously on a piece of paper.

'Well, I'm not sure, but – ' Milo stammered after several minutes of frantic calculating.

'You'll have to do better than that,' scolded the Dodecahedron, 'or you'll never know how far you've gone or whether or not you've ever got there.'

'I'm not very good at problems,' admitted Milo.

'What a shame,' sighed the Dodecahedron. 'They're so very useful. Why, did you know that if a beaver two feet long with a tail a foot and a half long can build a dam twelve feet high and six feet wide in two days, all you would need to build the Kariba Dam is a beaver sixty-eight feet long with a fifty-one-foot tail?'

'Where would you find a beaver as big as that?' grumbled the Humbug as his pencil point snapped.

'I'm sure I don't know,' he replied, 'but if you did, you'd certainly know what to do with him.'

'That's absurd,' objected Milo, whose head was spinning from all the numbers and questions.

'That may be true,' he acknowledged, 'but it's completely accurate, and as long as the answer is right, who cares if the question is wrong? If you want sense, you'll have to make it yourself.'

'All three roads arrive at the same place at the same time,' interrupted Tock, who had patiently been doing the first problem.

'Correct!' shouted the Dodecahedron. 'And I'll take you there myself. Now you can see how important problems are. If you hadn't done this one properly, you might have gone the wrong way.'

'I can't see where I made my mistake,' said the Humbug, frantically rechecking his figures.

'But if all the roads arrive at the same place at the same time, then aren't they all the right way?' asked Milo.

'Certainly not!' he shouted, glaring from his most upset face. 'They're all the *wrong* way. Just because you have a choice, it doesn't mean that any of them *has* to be right.'

He walked to the sign and quickly spun it around three times. As he did, the three roads vanished and a new one suddenly appeared, heading in the direction that the sign now pointed.

'Is every road five miles from Digitopolis?' asked Milo.

'I'm afraid it has to be,' the Dodecahedron replied, leaping on to the back of the car. 'It's the only sign we've got.'

The new road was quite bumpy and full of stones, and each time they hit one, the Dodecahedron bounced into the air and landed on one of his faces, with a sulk or a smile or a laugh or a frown, depending upon which one it was.

'We'll soon be there,' he announced happily, after one of his short flights. 'Welcome to the land of numbers.'

'It doesn't look very inviting,' the bug remarked, for, as they climbed higher and higher, not a tree or a blade of grass could be seen anywhere. Only the rocks remained.

'Is this the place where numbers are made?' asked Milo as the car lurched again, and this time the Dodecahedron sailed off down the mountainside, head over heels and grunt over grimace, until he landed sad side up at what looked like the entrance to a cave.

'They're not made,' he replied, as if nothing had happened. 'You have to dig for them. Don't you know anything at all about numbers?'

'Well, I don't think they're very important,' snapped Milo, too embarrassed to admit the truth.

'NOT IMPORTANT!' roared the Dodecahedron, turning red with fury. 'Could you have tea for two without the two – or three blind mice without the three? Would there be four corners of the earth if there weren't a four? And how could you sail the seven seas without a seven?'

'All I meant was——' began Milo, but the Dodecahedron, overcome with emotion and shouting furiously, carried on.

'If you had high hopes, how would you know how high they were? And did you know that narrow escapes come in all different widths? Would you travel the whole wide world without ever knowing how wide it was? And how could you do anything at long last,' he concluded, waving his arms over his head, 'without knowing how long the last was? Why, numbers are the most beautiful and valuable things in the world. Just follow me and I'll show you.' He turned on his heel and stalked off into the cave.

'Come along, come along,' he shouted from the dark hole. 'I can't wait for you all day.' And in a moment they'd followed him into the mountain.

It took several minutes for their eyes to become accustomed to the dim light, and during that time strange scratching, scraping, tapping, scuffling noises could be heard all around them.

'Put these on,' instructed the Dodecahedron, handing each of them a helmet with a flashlight attached to the top.

'Where are we going?' whispered Milo, for it seemed the kind of place in which you whispered.

'We're here,' he replied with a sweeping gesture. 'This is the numbers mine.'

Milo squinted into the darkness and saw for the first time that they had entered a vast cavern lit only by a soft, eerie glow from the great stalactites which hung ominously from the ceiling. Passages and corridors honeycombed the walls and wound their way from floor to ceiling, up and down the sides of the cave. And, everywhere he looked, Milo saw little men no bigger than himself busy digging and chopping, shovelling and scraping, pulling and tugging carts full of stone from one place to another.

'Right this way,' instructed the Dodecahedron, 'and watch where you step.'

As he spoke, his voice echoed and re-echoed and re-echoed again, mixing its sound with the buzz of activity all around them. Tock trotted along next to Milo, and the Humbug, stepping daintily, followed behind.

'Whose mine is it?' asked Milo, stepping around two of the loaded wagons.

'BY THE FOUR MILLION EIGHT HUNDRED AND TWENTY-SEVEN THOUSAND SIX HUNDRED AND FIFTY-NINE HAIRS ON MY HEAD, IT'S MINE, OF COURSE!' bellowed a voice from across the cavern. And striding towards them came a figure who could only have been a Mathemagician.

He was dressed in a long flowing robe covered entirely with complex mathematical equations and a tall pointed cap that made him look very wise. In his left hand he carried a long staff with a pencil point at one end and a large rubber eraser at the other.

'It's a lovely mine,' apologized the Humbug, who was always intimidated by loud noises.

'The biggest number mine in the kingdom,' said the Mathemagician proudly.

'Are there any precious stones in it?' asked Milo excitedly.

'PRECIOUS STONES!' he roared, even louder than before. And then he leaned over toward Milo and whispered softly, 'By the eight million two hundred and forty-seven thousand three hundred and twelve threads in my robe, I'll say there are. Look here.'

He reached into one of the carts and pulled out a small object, which he polished vigorously on his robe. When he held it up to the light, it sparkled brightly.

'But that's a five,' objected Milo, for that was certainly what it was.

'Exactly,' agreed the Mathemagician; 'as valuable a jewel as you'll find anywhere. Look at some of the others.'

He scooped up a great handful of stones and poured them into Milo's arms. They included all the numbers from one to nine, and even an assortment of zeros.

'We dig them and polish them in here,' volunteered the Dodecahedron, pointing to a group of workers busily employed at the buffing wheels; 'and then we send them all over the world. Marvellous, aren't they?'

'They are exceptional,' said Tock, who had a special fondness for numbers.

'So that's where they come from,' said Milo, looking in awe at the glittering collection of numbers. He returned them to the Dodecahedron as carefully as possible but, as he did, one dropped to the floor with a smash and broke in two. The Humbug winced and Milo looked terribly concerned.

'Oh, don't worry about that,' said the Mathemagician as he scooped up the pieces. 'We use the broken ones for fractions.'

'Haven't you any diamonds or emeralds or rubies?' asked

the bug irritably, for he was quite disappointed in what he'd seen so far.

'Yes, indeed,' the Mathemagician replied, leading them to the rear of the cave; 'come this way.'

There, piled into enormous mounds that reached almost to the ceiling, were not only diamonds and emeralds and rubies but also sapphires, amethysts, topazes, moonstones, and garnets. It was the most amazing mass of wealth that any of them had ever seen.

'They're such a terrible nuisance,' sighed the Mathemagician, 'and no one can think what to do with them. So we just keep digging them up and throwing them out. Now,' he said, taking a silver whistle from his pocket and blowing it loudly, 'let's have some lunch.'

And for the first time in his life the astonished bug couldn't think of a thing to say.

## 15 *This Way to Infinity*

Into the cavern rushed eight of the strongest miners carrying an immense cauldron which bubbled and sizzled and sent great clouds of savoury steam spiralling slowly to the ceiling. A sweet yet pungent aroma hung in the air and drifted easily from one anxious nose to the other, stopping only long enough to make several mouths water and a few stomachs growl. Milo, Tock, and the Humbug watched eagerly as the rest of the workers put down their tools and gathered round the big pot to help themselves.

'Perhaps you'd care for something to eat?' said the Mathemagician, offering each of them a heaping bowlful.

'Yes, sir,' said Milo, who was beside himself with hunger.

'Thank you,' added Tock.

The Humbug made no reply, for he was already too busy eating, and in a moment the three of them had finished absolutely everything they'd been given.

'Please have another portion,' said the Mathemagician, filling their bowls once more; and as quickly as they'd finished the first one the second was emptied too.

'Don't stop now,' he insisted, serving them again,
      and again,
            and again,
                  and again,
                        and again,
                            and again.

'How very strange,' thought Milo as he finished his seventh helping. 'Each one I eat makes me a little hungrier than the one before.'

'Do have some more,' suggested the Mathemagician, and they continued to eat just as fast as he filled the plates.

After Milo had eaten nine portions, Tock eleven, and the Humbug, without once stopping to look up, twenty-three, the Mathemagician blew his whistle for a second time and immediately the pot was removed and the miners returned to work.

'U-g-g-g-h-h-h,' gasped the bug, suddenly realizing that he was twenty-three times hungrier than when he started, 'I think I'm starving.'

'Me, too,' complained Milo, whose stomach felt as empty as he could ever remember; 'and I ate so much.'

'Yes, it was delicious, wasn't it?' agreed the pleased Dodecahedron, wiping the gravy from several of his mouths. 'It's the speciality of the kingdom – subtraction stew.'

'I have more of an appetite than when I began,' said Tock, leaning weakly against one of the larger rocks.

'Certainly,' replied the Mathemagician; 'what did you expect? The more you eat, the hungrier you get. Everyone knows that.'

'They do?' said Milo doubtfully. 'Then how do you ever get enough?'

'Enough?' he said impatiently. 'Here in Digitopolis we have our meals when we're full and eat until we're hungry. That way, when you don't have anything at all, you have more than enough. It's a very economical system. You must have been quite stuffed to have eaten so much.'

'It's completely logical,' explained the Dodecahedron. 'The more you want, the less you get, and the less you get, the more you have. Simple arithmetic, that's all. Suppose you had something and added something to it. What would that make?'

'More,' said Milo quickly.

'Quite correct,' he nodded. 'Now suppose you had something and added nothing to it. What would you have?'

'The same,' he answered again, without much conviction.

'Splendid,' cried the Dodecahedron. 'And suppose you had something and added less than nothing to it. What would you have then?'

'FAMINE!' roared the anguished Humbug, who suddenly realized that that was exactly what he'd eaten twenty-three bowls of.

'It's not as bad as all that,' said the Dodecahedron from his most sympathetic face. 'In a few hours you'll be nice and full again – just in time for dinner.'

'Oh dear,' said Milo sadly and softly. 'I only eat when I'm hungry.'

'What a curious idea,' said the Mathemagician, raising his staff over his head and scrubbing the rubber end back and forth several times on the ceiling. 'The next thing you'll have us believe is that you only sleep when you're tired.' And by the time he'd finished the sentence, the cavern, the miners, and the Dodecahedron had vanished, leaving just the four of them standing in the Mathemagician's workshop.

'I often find,' he casually explained to his dazed visitors, 'that the best way to get from one place to another is to rub everything out and begin again. Please make yourself at home.'

'Do you always travel that way?' asked Milo as he glanced curiously at the strange circular room, whose sixteen tiny arched windows corresponded exactly to the sixteen points of the compass. Around the entire circumference were numbers from nought to three hundred and sixty, marking the degrees of the circle, and on the floor, walls, tables, chairs, desks, cabinets, and ceiling were labels showing their heights, widths, depths, and distances to and from each other. To one side was a gigantic note pad set on an artist's easel, and from hooks and strings hung a collection of scales, rulers, measures, weights, tapes, and all sorts of other devices for measuring any number of things in every possible way.

'No indeed,' replied the Mathemagician, and this time he raised the sharpened end of his staff, drew a thin straight line in the air, and then walked gracefully across it from one side of the room to the other. 'Most of the time I take the shortest distance between any two points. And, of course, when I should be in several places at once,' he remarked, writing $7 \times 1 = 7$ carefully on the note pad, 'I simply multiply.'

Suddenly there were seven Mathemagicians standing side by side, and each one looked exactly like the other.

'How did you do that?' gasped Milo.

'There's nothing to it,' they all said in chorus, 'if you have a magic staff.' Then six of them cancelled themselves out and simply disappeared.

'But it's only a big pencil,' the Humbug objected, tapping at it with his cane.

'True enough,' agreed the Mathemagician; 'but once you learn to use it, there's no end to what you can do.'

'Can you make things disappear?' asked Milo excitedly.

'Why, certainly,' he said, striding over to the easel. 'Just step a little closer and watch carefully.'

After demonstrating that there was nothing up his sleeves, in his hat, or behind his back, he wrote quickly:

$$4 + 9 - 2 \times 16 + 1 \div 3 \times 6 - 67 + 8 \times 2 - 3 + 26 - 1 \div 34 + 3 \div 7 + 2 - 5 =$$

Then he looked up expectantly.

'Seventeen!' shouted the bug, who always managed to be first with the wrong answer.

'It all comes to nothing,' corrected Milo.

'Precisely,' said the Mathemagician, making a very theatrical bow, and the entire line of numbers vanished before their eyes. 'Now is there anything else you'd like to see?'

'Yes, please,' said Milo. 'Can you show me the biggest number there is?'

'I'd be delighted,' he replied, opening one of the cupboard doors. 'We keep it just here. It took four miners just to dig it out.'

Inside was the biggest

3

Milo had ever seen. It was fully twice as high as the Mathemagician.

'No, that's not what I mean,' objected Milo. 'Can you show me the longest number there is?'

'Surely,' said the Mathemagician, opening another door. 'Here it is. It took three carts to carry it here.'

And there was the longest

imaginable. It was just about as wide as the three was high.

'No, no, no, that's not what I mean either,' he said, looking helplessly at Tock.

'I think what you would like to see,' said the dog, scratching himself just under half-past four, 'is the number of greatest possible magnitude.'

'Well, why didn't you say so?' said the Mathemagician, who was busily measuring the edge of a raindrop. 'What's the greatest number *you* can think of?'

'Nine trillion, nine hundred ninety-nine billion, nine hundred ninety-nine million, nine hundred ninety-nine thousand, nine hundred ninety-nine,' recited Milo breathlessly.

'Very good,' said the Mathemagician. 'Now add one to it. Now add one again,' he repeated when Milo had added the previous one. 'Now add one again. Now add one again. Now add one again. Now add one again. Now add one again. Now add one again. Now add one again. Now add –'

'But when can I stop?' pleaded Milo.

'Never,' said the Mathemagician with a little smile, 'for the number you want is always at least one more than the number you've got, and it's so large that if you started saying it yesterday you wouldn't finish tomorrow.'

'Where could you ever find a number so big?' scoffed the Humbug.

'In the same place they have the smallest number there is,' he answered helpfully; 'and you know what that is.'

'Certainly,' said the bug, suddenly remembering something to do at the other end of the room.

'One one-millionth?' asked Milo, trying to think of the smallest fraction possible.

'Almost,' said the Mathemagician. 'Now divide it in half. Now divide it in half again. Now divide it in half again. Now divide it in half again. Now divide it in half again. Now divide it in half again. Now divide it in half again. Now divide it in half again. Now divide –'

'Oh dear,' shouted Milo, holding his hands to his ears, 'doesn't that ever stop either?'

'How can it,' said the Mathemagician, 'when you can always take half of whatever you have left until it's so small that if you started to say it right now you'd finish even before you began?'

'Where could you keep anything so tiny?' Milo asked, trying very hard to imagine such a thing.

The Mathemagician stopped what he was doing and explained simply, 'Why, in a box that's so small you can't see it – and that's kept in a drawer that's so small you can't see it, in a dresser that's so small you can't see it, in a house that's so small you can't see it, on a street that's so small you can't see it, in a city that's so small you can't see it, which is part of a country that's so small you can't see it, in a world that's so small you can't see it.'

Then he sat down, fanned himself with a handkerchief, and continued. 'Then, of course, we keep the whole thing in another box that's so small you can't see it – and, if you follow me, I'll show you where to find it.'

They walked to one of the small windows and there, tied to the sill, was one end of a line that stretched along the ground and into the distance until completely out of sight.

'Just follow that line for ever,' said the Mathemagician, 'and when you reach the end, turn left. There you'll find the land of Infinity, where the tallest, the shortest, the biggest, the smallest, and the most and the least of everything are kept.'

'I really don't have much time,' said Milo anxiously. 'Isn't there a quicker way?'

'Well, you might try this flight of stairs,' he suggested, opening another door and pointing up. 'It goes there, too.'

Milo bounded across the room and started up the stairs two at a time. 'Wait for me, please,' he shouted to Tock and the Humbug. 'I'll be gone only a few minutes.'

## 16     *A Very Dirty Bird*

Up he went – very quickly at first – then more slowly – then in a little while even more slowly than that – and finally, after many minutes of climbing up the endless stairway, one weary foot was barely able to follow the other. Milo suddenly realized that with all his effort he was no closer to the top than when he began, and not a great deal farther from the bottom. But he struggled on for a little longer, until at last, completely exhausted, he collapsed on to one of the steps.

'I should have known it,' he mumbled, resting his tired legs and filling his lungs with air. 'This is just like the line that goes on for ever, and I'll never get there.'

'You wouldn't like it much anyway,' someone replied gently. 'Infinity is a dreadfully poor place. They can never manage to make ends meet.'

Milo looked up, with his head still resting heavily in his hand; he was becoming quite accustomed to being addressed at the oddest times, in the oddest places, by the oddest people – and this time he was not at all disappointed. Standing next to him on the step was exactly one half of a small child who had been divided neatly from top to bottom.

'Pardon me for staring,' said Milo, after he had been staring for some time, 'but I've never seen half a child before.'

'It's ·58 to be precise,' replied the child from the left side of his mouth (which happened to be the only side of his mouth).

'I beg your pardon?' said Milo.

'It's ·58,' he repeated; 'it's a little bit *more* than a half.'

'Have you always been like that?' asked Milo impatiently, for he felt that that was a needlessly fine distinction.

'My goodness, no,' the child assured him. 'A few years ago I was just ·42 and, believe me, that was terribly inconvenient.'

'What is the rest of your family like?' said Milo, this time a bit more sympathetically.

'Oh, we're just the average family,' he said thoughtfully; 'mother, father, and 2·58 children – and, as I explained, I'm the ·58.'

'It must be rather odd being only part of a person,' Milo remarked.

'Not at all,' said the child. 'Every average family has 2·58 children, so I always have someone to play with. Besides, each family also has an average of 1·3 automobiles, and since I'm the only one who can drive three tenths of a car, I can have the sole use of it.'

'But averages aren't real,' objected Milo; 'they're just imaginary.'

'That may be so,' he agreed, 'but they're also very useful at times. For instance, if you didn't have any money at all, but you happened to be with four other people who had ten dollars apiece, then you'd each have an average of eight dollars. Isn't that right?'

'I suppose so,' said Milo weakly.

'Well, think how much better off you'd be, just because of averages,' he explained convincingly. 'And think of the poor farmer when it doesn't rain all year: if there wasn't an average yearly rainfall of 37 inches in this part of the country, all his crops would wither and die.'

It all sounded terribly confusing to Milo, for he had always had trouble in school with this very subject.

'There are still other advantages,' continued the child. 'For instance, if one rat were cornered by nine cats, then, on the average, each cat would be 10 per cent rat and the rat would be 90 per cent cat. If you happened to be a rat, you can see how much nicer it would make things.'

'But that can never be,' said Milo, jumping to his feet.

'Don't be too sure,' said the child patiently, 'for one of the nicest things about mathematics, or anything else you might care to learn, is that many of the things which can never be, often are. You see,' he went on, 'it's very much like your trying to reach Infinity. You know that it's there, but you just don't know where – but just because you can never reach it doesn't mean that it's not worth looking for.'

'I hadn't thought of it that way,' said Milo, starting down the stairs. 'I think I'll go back now.'

'A wise decision,' the child agreed; 'but try again some day – perhaps you'll get much closer.' And, as Milo waved good-bye, he smiled warmly, which he usually did on an average of 47 times a day.

'Everyone here knows so much more than I do,' thought Milo, as he leaped from step to step. 'I'll have to do a lot better if I'm going to rescue the princesses.'

In a few moments he'd reached the bottom again and burst into the workshop, where Tock and the Humbug were eagerly watching the Mathemagician perform.

'Ah, back already,' he cried, greeting him with a friendly wave. 'I hope you found what you were looking for.'

'I'm afraid not,' admitted Milo. And then he added in a very discouraged tone, 'Everything in Digitopolis is much too difficult for me.'

The Mathemagician nodded knowingly and stroked his chin several times. 'You'll find,' he remarked gently, 'that the only thing you can do easily is be wrong, and that's hardly worth the effort.'

Milo tried very hard to understand all the things he'd been told, and all the things he'd seen, and, as he spoke, one curious thing still bothered him. 'Why is it,' he said quietly, 'that quite often even the things which are correct just don't seem to be right?'

A look of deep melancholy crossed the Mathemagician's face and his eyes grew moist with sadness. Everything was silent, and it was several minutes before he was able to reply at all.

'How very true,' he sobbed, supporting himself on the staff. 'It has been like that since Rhyme and Reason were banished.'

'Quite so,' began the Humbug. 'I personally feel that –'

'AND ALL BECAUSE OF THAT STUBBORN WRETCH AZAZ,' roared the Mathemagician, completely overwhelming the bug, for now his sadness had changed to fury and he stalked about the room adding up anger and multiplying wrath. 'IT'S ALL HIS FAULT.'

'Perhaps if you discussed it with him –' Milo started to say, but never had time to finish.

'He's much too unreasonable,' interrupted the Mathemagician again. 'Why, just last month I sent him a very friendly letter, which he never had the courtesy to answer. See for yourself.'

He handed Milo a copy of the letter, which read:

```
    4738    1919,
      667    394017    5841    62589
  85371      14     39588    7190434      203
  27689    57131    481206.
                          5864    98053,
                          62179875073
```

'But maybe he doesn't understand numbers,' said Milo, who found it a little difficult to read himself.

'NONSENSE!' he bellowed. 'Everyone understands numbers. No matter what language you speak, they always mean the same thing. A seven is a seven anywhere in the world.'

'My goodness,' thought Milo, 'everybody is so terribly sensitive about the things they know best.'

'With your permission,' said Tock, changing the subject, 'we'd like to rescue Rhyme and Reason.'

'Has Azaz agreed to it?' the Mathemagician inquired.

'Yes, sir,' the dog assured him.

'THEN I DON'T,' he thundered again, 'for since they've been banished, we've never agreed on anything – and we never will.' He emphasized his last remark with a dark and ominous look.

'Never?' asked Milo, with the slightest touch of disbelief in his voice.

'NEVER!' he repeated. 'And if you can prove otherwise, you have my permission to go.'

'Well,' said Milo, who had thought about this problem very carefully ever since leaving Dictionopolis.

'Then with whatever Azaz agrees, you disagree.'

'Correct,' said the Mathemagician with a tolerant smile.

'And with whatever Azaz disagrees, you agree.'

'Also correct,' yawned the Mathemagician, nonchalantly cleaning his fingernails with the point of his staff.

'Then each of you agrees that he will disagree with whatever each of you agrees with,' said Milo triumphantly; 'and if you both disagree with the same thing then aren't you really in agreement?'

'I'VE BEEN TRICKED!' cried the Mathemagician helplessly, for no matter how he worked it out, it still came out just like that.

'Splendid effort,' commented the Humbug jovially; 'exactly the way I would have done it myself.'

'And now may we go?' added Tock.

The Mathemagician accepted his defeat with grace, nodded weakly, and then drew the three travellers to his side.

'It's a long and dangerous journey,' he began softly, and a furrow of concern creased his forehead. 'Long before you find them, the demons will know you're there. Watch for them well,' he emphasized, 'for when they appear, it might be too late.'

The Humbug shuddered down to his shoes, and Milo felt the tips of his fingers suddenly grow cold.

'But there is one problem even more serious than that,' he whispered ominously.

'What is it?' gasped Milo, who was not sure he really wanted to know.

'I'm afraid I can tell you only when you return. Come along,' said the Mathemagician, 'and I'll show you the way.' And, simply by carrying the three, he transported them all to the very edge of Digitopolis. Behind them lay all the kingdoms of Wisdom, and up ahead a narrow rutted path led towards the mountains and darkness.

'We'll never get the car up that,' said Milo unhappily.

'True enough,' replied the Mathemagician, 'but you can be in Ignorance fast enough without riding all the way; and if you're to be successful, it will have to be step by step.'

'But I *would* like to take my gifts,' he insisted.

'So you shall,' announced the Dodecahedron, who appeared from nowhere with his arms full. 'Here are your sights, here are your sounds, and here,' he said, handing Milo the last of them disdainfully, 'are your words.'

'And, most important of all,' added the Mathemagician, 'here is your own magic staff. Use it well and there is nothing it cannot do for you.'

He placed in Milo's breast pocket a small gleaming pencil which, except for the size, was much like his own. Then, with a last word of encouragement, he and the Dodecahedron (who was simultaneously sobbing, frowning, pining, and sighing from four of his saddest faces) made their farewells and watched as the three tiny figures disappeared into the forbidding Mountains of Ignorance.

Almost immediately the light began to fade as the difficult path wandered aimlessly upward, inching forward almost as reluctantly as the trembling Humbug. Tock as usual led the way, sniffing ahead for danger, and Milo, his bag of precious possessions slung over one shoulder, followed silently and resolutely behind.

'Perhaps someone should stay behind to guard the way,' said the unhappy bug, offering his services; but, since his suggestion was met with silence, he followed glumly along.

The higher they went, the darker it became, though it wasn't the darkness of night, but rather more like a mixture of lurking shadows and evil intentions which oozed from the slimy moss-covered cliffs and blotted out the light. A cruel

wind shrieked through the rocks and the air was thick and heavy, as if it had been used several times before.

On they went, higher and higher up the dizzying trail, on one side the sheer stone walls and brutal peaks towering above them, and on the other an endless, limitless, bottomless nothing.

'I can hardly see a thing,' said Milo, taking hold of Tock's tail as a sticky mist engulfed the moon. 'Perhaps we should wait until morning.'

'They'll be mourning for you soon enough,' came a reply from directly above, and this was followed by a hideous cackling laugh very much like someone choking on a fish-bone.

Clinging to one of the greasy rocks and blending almost perfectly with it was a large, unkempt, and exceedingly soiled bird who looked more like a dirty floor mop than anything else. He had a sharp, dangerous beak, and the one eye he chose to open stared down maliciously.

'I don't think you understand,' said Milo timidly as the watchdog growled a warning. 'We're looking for a place to spend the night.'

'It's not yours to spend,' the bird shrieked again, and followed it with the same horrible laugh.

'That doesn't make any sense, you see –' he started to explain.

'Dollars or cents, it's still not yours to spend,' the bird replied haughtily.

'But I didn't mean –' insisted Milo.

'Of course you're mean,' interrupted the bird, closing the eye that had been open and opening the one that had been closed. 'Anyone who'd spend a night that doesn't belong to him is very mean.'

'Well, I thought that by –' he tried again desperately.

'That's a different story,' interjected the bird a bit more amiably. 'If you want to buy, I'm sure I can arrange to sell, but with what you're doing you'll probably end up in a cell anyway.'

'That doesn't seem right,' said Milo helplessly, for, with the bird taking everything the wrong way, he hardly knew what he was saying.

'Agreed,' said the bird, with a sharp click of his beak, 'but neither is it left, although if I were you I would have left a long time ago.'

'Let me try once more,' he said in an effort to explain. 'In other words –'

'You mean you have other words?' cried the bird happily. 'Well, by all means, use them. You're certainly not doing very well with the ones you have now.'

'Must you always interrupt like that?' said Tock irritably, for even he was becoming impatient.

'Naturally,' he cackled; 'it's my job. I take the words right out of your mouth. Haven't we met before? I'm the Everpresent Wordsnatcher, and I'm sure I know your friend the bug.' And then he leaned all the way forward and gave a terrible knowing smile.

The Humbug, who was too big to hide and too frightened to move, denied everything.

'Is everyone who lives in Ignorance like you?' asked Milo.

'Much worse,' he said longingly. 'But I don't live here. I'm from a place very far away called Context.'

'Don't you think you should be getting back?' suggested the bug, holding one arm up in front of him.

'What a horrible thought.' The bird shuddered. 'It's such an unpleasant place that I spend almost all my time out of it. Besides, what could be nicer than these grimy mountains?'

'Almost anything,' thought Milo as he pulled his collar up. And then he asked the bird, 'Are you a demon?'

'I'm afraid not,' he replied sadly, as several filthy tears rolled down his beak. 'I've tried, but the best I can manage to be is a nuisance,' and, before Milo could reply, he flapped his dingy wings and flew off in a cascade of dust and dirt and fuzz.

'Wait!' shouted Milo, who'd thought of many more questions he wanted to ask.

'Thirty-four pounds,' shrieked the bird as he disappeared into the fog.

'He was certainly no help,' said Milo after they had been walking again for some time.

'That's why I drove him off,' cried the Humbug, fiercely brandishing his cane. 'Now let's find the demons.'

'That might be sooner than you think,' remarked Tock, looking back at the suddenly trembling bug; and the trail turned again and continued to climb.

In a few minutes they'd reached the crest, only to find that beyond it lay another one even higher, and beyond that several more, whose tops were lost in the swirling darkness. For a short stretch the path became broad and flat, and just ahead, leaning comfortably against a dead tree, stood a very elegant-looking gentleman.

He was beautifully dressed in a dark suit with a well-pressed shirt and tie. His shoes were polished, his nails were clean, his hat was well brushed, and a white handkerchief

adorned his breast pocket. But his expression was somewhat blank. In fact, it was completely blank, for he had neither eyes, nose, nor mouth.

'Hello, little boy,' he said, amiably shaking Milo by the hand. 'And how's the faithful dog?' he inquired, giving Tock three or four strong and friendly pats. 'And who is this handsome creature?' he asked, tipping his hat to the very pleased Humbug. 'I'm so happy to see you all.'

'What a pleasant surprise to meet someone so nice,' they all thought, 'and especially here.'

'I wonder if you could spare me a little of your time,' he inquired politely, 'and help with a few small jobs?'

'Why, of course,' said the Humbug cheerfully.

'Gladly,' added Tock.

'Yes, indeed,' said Milo, who wondered for just a moment how it was possible for someone so agreeable to have a face with no features at all.

'Splendid,' he said happily, 'for there are just three tasks. Firstly, I would like to move this pile from here to there,' he explained, pointing to an enormous mound of fine sand; 'but I'm afraid that all I have is this tiny pair of tweezers.' And he gave them to Milo, who immediately began transporting one grain at a time.

'Secondly, I would like to empty this well and fill the other; but I have no bucket, so you'll have to use this eye-dropper.' And he handed it to Tock, who undertook at once to carry one drop at a time from well to well.

'And, lastly, I must have a hole through this cliff, and here is a needle to dig it.' The eager Humbug quickly set to work picking at the solid granite wall.

When they had all been safely started, the very pleasant man returned to the tree and, leaning against it once more, continued to stare vacantly down the trail, while Milo, Tock,

and the Humbug worked hour after hour after hour after hour after hour after hour after hour after hour after hour after hour after hour after hour after hour after hour after hour after hour after hour after hour after hour after hour after hour –

# 17  *Unwelcoming Committee*

The Humbug whistled gaily at his work, for he was never as happy as when he had a job which required no thinking at all. After what seemed like days, he had dug a hole scarcely large enough for his thumb. Tock shuffled steadily back and forth with the dropper in his teeth, but the full well was still almost as full as when he began, and Milo's new pile of sand was hardly a pile at all.

'How very strange,' said Milo, without stopping for a moment. 'I've been working steadily all this time, and I don't feel the slightest bit tired or hungry. I could go right on the same way for ever.'

'Perhaps you will,' the man agreed with a yawn (at least it sounded like a yawn).

'Well, I wish I knew how long it was going to take,' Milo whispered as the dog went by again.

'Why not use your magic staff and find out?' replied Tock as clearly as anyone could with an eye-dropper in his mouth.

Milo took the shiny pencil from his pocket and quickly calculated that, at the rate they were working, it would take each of them eight hundred and thirty-seven years to finish.

'Pardon me,' he said, tugging at the man's sleeve and holding the sheet of figures up for him to see, 'but it's going to take eight hundred and thirty-seven years to do these jobs.'

'Is that so?' replied the man, without even turning round. 'Well, you'd better get on with it then.'

'But it hardly seems worth while,' said Milo softly.

'WORTH WHILE!' the man roared indignantly.

'All I meant was that perhaps it isn't too important,' Milo repeated, trying not to be impolite.

'Of course it's not important,' he snarled angrily. 'I wouldn't have asked you to do it if I thought it was important.' And now, as he turned to face them, he didn't seem quite so pleasant.

'Then why bother?' asked Tock, whose alarm suddenly began to ring.

'Because, my young friends,' he muttered sourly, 'what could be more important than doing unimportant things? If you stop to do enough of them, you'll never get to where you're going.' He punctuated his last remark with a villainous laugh.

'Then you must –' gasped Milo.

'Quite correct!' he shrieked triumphantly. 'I am the Terrible Trivium, demon of petty tasks and worthless jobs, ogre of wasted effort, and monster of habit.'

The Humbug dropped his needle and stared in disbelief while Milo and Tock began to back away slowly.

'Don't try to leave,' he ordered, with a menacing sweep of his arm, 'for there's so very much to do, and you still have over eight hundred years to go on the first job.'

'But why do only unimportant things?' asked Milo, who suddenly remembered how much time he spent each day doing them.

'Think of all the trouble it saves,' the man explained, and his face looked as if he'd be grinning an evil grin – if he could grin at all. 'If you only do the easy and useless jobs, you'll never have to worry about the important ones which are so difficult. You just won't have the time. For there's always something to do to keep you from what you really should be doing, and if it weren't for that dreadful magic staff, you'd never know how much time you were wasting.'

As he spoke, he tiptoed slowly towards them with his arms outstretched and continued to whisper in a soft, deceitful voice, 'Now do come and stay with me. We'll have so much fun together. There are things to fill and things to empty, things to take away and things to bring back, things to pick up and things to put down, and besides all that we have pencils to sharpen, holes to dig, nails to straighten, stamps to lick, and ever so much more. Why, if you stay here, you'll never have to think again – and with a little practice you can become a monster of habit, too.'

They were all transfixed by the Trivium's soothing voice, but just as he was about to clutch them in his well-manicured fingers a voice cried out, 'RUN! RUN!'

Milo, who thought it was Tock, turned suddenly and dashed up the trail.

'RUN! RUN!' it shouted again, and this time Tock thought it was Milo and quickly followed him.

'RUN! RUN!' it urged once more, and now the Humbug, not caring who said it, ran desperately after his two friends, with the Terrible Trivium close behind.

'This way! This way!' the voice called again. They turned in its direction and scrambled up the difficult slippery rocks, sliding back at each step almost as far as they'd gone forward. With a great effort and many helping paws from Tock, they reached the top of the ridge at last, but only two steps ahead of the furious Trivium.

'Over here! Over here!' advised the voice, and without a moment's hesitation they started through a puddle of sticky ooze, which quickly became ankle-deep, then knee-deep, then hip-deep, until finally they were struggling along through what felt very much like a waist-deep pool of peanut butter.

The Trivium, who had discovered a mound of pebbles

which needed counting, followed no more, but stood at the edge shaking his fist, shouting horrible threats, and promising to rouse every demon in the mountains.

'What a nasty fellow,' gasped Milo, who was having great difficulty just getting his legs to move. 'I hope I never meet him again.'

'I believe he's stopped chasing us,' said the bug, looking back over his shoulder.

'It's not what's behind that worries me,' remarked Tock as they stepped from the sticky mess, 'but what's ahead.'

'Keep going straight! Keep going straight!' advised the voice as they continued to pick their way carefully along the new path.

'Now step up! Now step up!' it recommended, and almost before they knew what had happened, they had all taken a step up and then plunged to the bottom of a deep murky pit.

'But he said *up*!' Milo complained bitterly from where he lay sprawling.

'Well, I hope you didn't expect to get anywhere by listening to me,' said the voice gleefully.

'We'll never get out of here,' the Humbug moaned, looking at the steep, smooth sides of the pit.

'That is quite an accurate evaluation of the situation,' said the voice coldly.

'Then why did you help us at all?' shouted Milo angrily.

'Oh, I'd do as much for anybody,' he replied; 'bad advice is my speciality. For, as you can plainly see, I'm the long-nosed, green-eyed, curly-haired, wide-mouthed, thick-necked, broad-shouldered, round-bodied, short-armed, bow-legged, big-footed monster – and, if I do say so myself, one of the most frightening fiends in this whole wild wilderness. With me here, you wouldn't dare try to escape.' And, with that, he shuffled to the edge of the pit and leered down at his helpless prisoners.

Tock and the Humbug turned away in fright, but Milo,

who had learned by now that people are not always what they say they are, reached for his telescope and took a long look for himself. And there at the rim of the hole, instead of what he'd expected, stood a small furry creature with very worried eyes and a rather sheepish grin.

'Why, you're not long-nosed, green-eyed, curly-haired, wide-mouthed, thick-necked, broad-shouldered, round-bodied, short-armed, bowlegged, or big-footed – and you're not at all frightening,' said Milo indignantly. 'What kind of a demon are you?'

The little creature, who seemed stunned at being found out, leaped back out of sight and began to whimper softly.

'I'm the demon of insincerity,' he sobbed. 'I don't mean what I say, I don't mean what I do, and I don't mean what I am. Most people who believe what I tell them go the wrong way, and stay there, but you and your awful telescope have spoiled everything. I'm going home.' And, crying hysterically, he stamped off in a huff.

'It certainly pays to have a good look at things,' observed Milo as he wrapped up the telescope with great care.

'Now all we have to do is climb out,' said Tock, placing his front paws as high on the wall as he could. 'Here, hop up on my back.'

Milo climbed on to the dog's shoulders. Then the bug crawled up both of them and, by standing on Milo's head, just managed to hook his cane on the root of an old gnarled tree. With loud complaints he hung on doggedly until the other two had climbed out over him and pulled him up, somewhat dazed and discouraged.

'I'll lead the way for a while,' he said, brushing himself off. 'Follow me and we'll stay out of trouble.'

He guided them along one of five narrow ledges, all of which led to a grooved and rutted plateau. They stopped for a moment to rest and make plans, but before they had done either the whole mountain trembled violently and, with a sudden lurch, rose high into the air carrying them along with it. For, quite accidentally, they had stepped into the calloused hand of the Gelatinous Giant.

'AND WHAT HAVE WE HERE?' he roared, looking curiously at the tiny figures huddled in his palm – and licking his lips.

He was an incredible size even sitting down, with long unkempt hair, bulging eyes, and a shape hardly worth speaking of. He looked, in fact, very much like a colossal bowl of jelly, without the bowl.

'HOW DARE YOU DISTURB MY NAP!' he bellowed furiously, and the force of his hot breath tumbled them over in his hand.

'We're terribly sorry,' said Milo meekly, when he'd untangled himself, 'but you looked just like part of the mountain.'

'Naturally,' the giant replied in a more normal voice (but even this was like an explosion). 'I have no shape of my own,

so I try to be just like whatever I'm near. In the mountains I'm a lofty peak, on the beach a broad sand bar, in the forest a towering oak, and sometimes in the city I'm a very handsome twelve-story block of flats. I just hate to be conspicuous; it's really not safe, you know.' Then he looked at them again with hungry eyes and wondered how good they'd taste.

'You look much too big to be afraid of anything,' said Milo quickly, for the giant had already begun to open his mouth wide.

'I'm not,' he said, with a slight shiver that ran all over his gelatinous body. 'I'm afraid of everything. That's why I'm so ferocious. If the others found out, I'd just die. Now do be quiet while I eat my breakfast.' He raised his hand towards his gaping mouth and the Humbug shut his eyes tightly and clasped both hands over his head.

'Then aren't you really a fearful demon?' Milo asked desperately, on the assumption that the giant had been brought up well enough not to talk with a mouthful.

'Well, approximately yes,' he replied, lowering his arm to the vast relief of the bug; 'that is, comparatively no. What I mean is, relatively maybe – in other words, roughly perhaps. What does everyone else think? There, you see,' he said peevishly; 'I'm even afraid to make a positive statement. So please stop asking questions before I lose my appetite altogether.' Then he raised his arm again and prepared to swallow the three of them in one gulp.

'Why don't you help us rescue Rhyme and Reason? Then maybe things will get better,' shouted Milo again, this time almost too late, for in another instant they would have all been gone.

'Oh, I wouldn't do that,' said the giant thoughtfully, lowering his arm once more. 'I mean, why not leave well enough alone? That is, it'll never work. I wouldn't take a chance. In other words, let's keep things as they are – changes are so frightening.' As he spoke he began to look a bit ill.

'Maybe I'll just eat one of you,' he remarked unhappily, 'and save the rest for later. I don't feel very well.'

'I have a better idea,' said Milo.

'You have?' interrupted the giant, losing any desire to eat at all. 'If it's one thing I can't swallow, it's ideas: they're so hard to digest.'

'I have a box full of all the ideas in the world,' said Milo, proudly holding up the gift King Azaz had given him.

The thought of it terrified the giant, who began to shake like an enormous pudding.

'PUT ME DOWN AND JUST GO AWAY,' he pleaded, forgetting for a moment who had hold of whom; 'AND PLEASE DON'T OPEN THAT BOX!'

In another moment he'd set them down on the next jagged peak and, with panic in his eyes, lumbered off to warn the others of this terrible new threat.

But news travels quickly. The Wordsnatcher, the Trivium, and the long-nosed, green-eyed, curly-haired, wide-mouthed, thick-necked, broad-shouldered, round-bodied, short-armed, bowlegged, big-footed monster had already spread the alarm throughout the evil, unenlightened mountains.

And out the demons came – from every cave and crevice, through every fissure and crack, from under the rocks and up from the mud, stomping and shuffling, slithering and sliding, through the murky shadows. And all had only one thought in mind: destroy the intruders and protect Ignorance.

From where they stood, Milo, Tock, and the Humbug could see them moving steadily forward, still far away, but coming quickly. On all sides the cliffs were alive with this collection of crawling, looming, creeping, lurching shapes. Some could be seen plainly, others were but dim silhouettes, and yet still more, only now beginning to stir from their foul places, would be along much sooner than they were wanted.

'We'd better hurry,' barked Tock, 'or they're sure to catch us.' And he started up the trail again.

Milo took one deep breath and did the same; and the bug, now that he knew what lay behind, ran ahead with renewed enthusiasm.

## 18　Castle in the Air

Higher and higher they climbed, in search of the castle and the two banished princesses – from one crest to the next, from jagged rock to jagged rock, up frightful crumbling cliffs and along desperately narrow ledges where a single mis-step meant only good-bye. An ominous silence dropped like a curtain around them and, except for the scuffling of their frantic footsteps, there wasn't a sound. The world that Milo knew was a million thoughts away, and the demons – the demons were *there* in the distance.

'They're gaining!' shouted the Humbug, wishing he'd never looked back.

'But there it is!' cried Milo at the same instant, for straight ahead, climbing up from atop the highest peak, was a spidery spiral stair, and at the other end stood the Castle in the Air.

'I see it, I see it,' said the happy bug as they struggled up the twisting mountain trail. But what he didn't see was that, curled up right in front of the first step, was a little round man in a frock coat, sleeping peacefully on a very large and well-worn ledger.

A long quill pen sat precariously behind his ear, there were inkstains all over his hands and face as well as his clothing, and he wore a pair of the thickest eye-glasses that Milo had ever seen.

'Be very careful,' whispered Tock when they'd finally reached the top, and the Humbug stepped gingerly around and started up the stairs.

'NAMES?' the little man called out briskly, just as the startled bug reached the first step. He sat up quickly, pulled the book out from under him, put on a green eye-shade, and waited with his pen poised in the air.

'Well, I –' stammered the bug.

'NAMES?' he cried again, and as he did he opened the book to page 512 and began to write furiously. The quill made horrible scratching noises, and the point, which was continually catching in the paper, flicked tiny inkblots all over him. As they called out their names, he noted them carefully in alphabetical order.

'Splendid, splendid, splendid,' he muttered to himself. 'I haven't had an M for ages.'

'What do you want our names for?' asked Milo, looking anxiously over his shoulder. 'We're in a bit of a hurry.'

'Oh, this won't take a minute,' the man assured them. 'I'm the official Senses Taker, and I must have some information before I can take your senses. Now, if you'll just tell me when you were born, where you were born, why you were born, how old you are now, how old you were then, how old you'll be in a little while, your mother's name, your father's name, your aunt's name, your uncle's name, your cousin's name, where you live, how long you've lived there, the schools you've attended, the schools you haven't attended, your hobbies, your telephone number, your shoe size, shirt size, collar size, hat size, and the names and addresses of six people who can verify all this information, we'll get started. One at a time, please; stand in line; and no pushing, no talking, no peeking.'

The Humbug, who had difficulty remembering anything, went first. The little man leisurely recorded each answer in five different places, pausing often to polish his glasses, clear his throat, straighten his tie, and blow his nose. He managed also to cover the distressed bug in ink from head to foot.

'NEXT!' he announced very officially.

'I do wish he'd hurry,' said Milo, stepping forward, for in the distance he could see the first of the demons already beginning to scale the mountain towards them, no more than a few minutes away.

The little man wrote with painful deliberation, finally finished with both Milo and Tock, and looked up happily.

'May we go now?' asked the dog, whose sensitive nose had picked up a loathsome, evil smell that grew stronger every second.

'By all means,' said the man agreeably, 'just as soon as you finish telling me your height; your weight; the number of books you read each year; the number of books you don't read each year; the amount of time you spend eating, playing, working, and sleeping every day; where you go for your holidays; how many ice-cream cones you eat in a week; and which is your favourite colour. Then, after that, please fill out these forms and applications – three copies of each – and be careful, for if you make one mistake, you'll have to do them all over again.'

'Oh dear,' said Milo, looking at the pile of papers, 'we'll never finish these.' And even as he spoke the demons swarmed stealthily up the mountain.

'Come, come,' said the Senses Taker, chuckling gaily to himself, 'don't take all day. I'm expecting several more visitors any minute now.'

They set to work feverishly on the difficult forms, and when they'd finished, Milo placed them all in the little man's lap. He thanked them politely, took off his eye-shade, put the pen behind his ear, closed the book, and went back to sleep. The Humbug took one horrified look back over his shoulder and quickly started up the stairs.

'DESTINATION?' shouted the Senses Taker, sitting up again, putting on his eyeshade, taking the pen from behind his ear, and opening his book.

'But I thought –' protested the astonished bug.

'DESTINATION?' he repeated, making several notations in the ledger.

'The Castle in the Air,' said Milo impatiently.

'Why bother?' said the Senses Taker, pointing into the distance. 'I'm sure you'd rather see what I have to show you.'

As he spoke, they all looked up, but only Milo could see the gay and exciting circus there on the horizon. There were tents and side-shows and rides and even wild animals – everything a little boy could spend hours watching.

'And wouldn't you enjoy a more pleasant aroma?' he said, turning to Tock.

Almost immediately the dog smelled a wonderful smell that no one but he could smell. It was made up of all the marvellous things that had ever delighted his curious nose.

'And here's something I know you'll enjoy hearing,' he assured the Humbug.

The bug listened with rapt attention to something he alone could hear – the shouts and applause of an enormous crowd, all cheering for him.

They each stood as if in a trance, looking, smelling, and listening to the very special things that the Senses Taker had provided for them, forgetting completely about where they were going and who, with evil intent, was coming up behind them.

The Senses Taker sat back with a satisfied smile on his puffy little face as the demons came closer and closer, until less than a minute separated them from their helpless victims.

But Milo was too engrossed in the circus to notice, and Tock had closed his eyes, the better to smell, and the bug, bowing and waving, stood with a look of sheer bliss on his face, interested only in the wild ovation.

The little man had done his work well and, except for some ominous crawling noises just below the crest of the mountain, everything was again silent. Milo, who stood staring blankly into the distance, let his bag of gifts slip from his shoulder to the ground. And, as he did, the package of sounds broke open, filling the air with peals of happy laughter which seemed so gay that first he, then Tock, and finally the Humbug joined in. And suddenly the spell was broken.

'There is no circus,' cried Milo, realizing he'd been tricked.

'There were no smells,' barked Tock, his alarm now ringing furiously.

'The applause is gone,' complained the disappointed Humbug.

'I warned you; I warned you I was the Senses Taker,' sneered the Senses Taker. 'I help people find what they're *not* looking for, hear what they're *not* listening for, run after what they're *not* chasing, and smell what isn't even there. And, furthermore,' he cackled, hopping around gleefully on his stubby legs, 'I'll steal your sense of purpose, take your sense of duty, destroy your sense of proportion – and, but for one thing, you'd be helpless yet.'

'What's that?' asked Milo fearfully.

'As long as you have the sound of laughter,' he groaned unhappily, 'I cannot take your sense of humour – and, with it, you've nothing to fear from me.'

'But what about THEM?' cried the terrified bug, for at that very instant the other demons had reached the top at last and were leaping forward to seize them.

They ran for the stairs, bowling over the disconsolate Senses Taker, ledger, ink bottle, eyeshade, and all, as they went. The Humbug dashed up first, then Tock, and lastly Milo, almost too late, as a scaly arm brushed his shoe.

The dangerous stairs danced dizzily in the wind, and the clumsy demons refused to follow; but they howled with rage and fury, swore bloody vengeance, and watched with many pairs of burning eyes as the three small shapes vanished slowly into the clouds.

'Don't look down,' advised Milo as the bug tottered upward on unsteady legs.

Like a giant corkscrew, the stairway twisted through the darkness, steep and narrow and with no rail to guide them. The wind howled cruelly in an effort to tear them loose, and the fog dragged clammy fingers down their backs; but up the giddy flight they went, each one helping the others, until at last the clouds parted, the darkness fell away, and a glow of golden sunrays warmed their arrival. The castle gate swung smoothly open, and on a rug as soft as a snowdrift they entered the great hall and they stood shyly waiting.

'Come in, please; we've been expecting you,' sang out two sweet voices in unison.

At the far end of the hall a silver curtain parted and two young women stepped forward. They were dressed all in white and were beautiful beyond compare. One was grave and quiet, with a look of warm understanding in her eyes, and the other seemed gay and joyful.

'You must be the Princess of Pure Reason,' said Milo, bowing to the first.

She answered simply, 'Yes,' and that was just enough.

'Then you are Sweet Rhyme,' he said, with a smile to the other.

Her eyes sparkled brightly and she answered with a laugh as friendly as the postman's ring when you know there's a letter for you.

'We've come to rescue you both,' Milo explained very seriously.

'And the demons are close behind,' said the worried Humbug, still shaky from his ordeal.

'And we should leave immediately,' advised Tock.

'Oh, they won't dare come up here,' said Reason gently; 'and we'll be down there soon enough.'

'Why not sit for a moment and rest?' suggested Rhyme. 'I'm sure you must be tired. Have you been travelling long?'

'Days,' sighed the exhausted dog, curling up on a large downy cushion.

'Weeks,' corrected the bug, flopping into a deep comfortable arm-chair, for it did seem like that to him.

'It *has* been a long trip,' said Milo, climbing on to the couch where the princesses sat; 'but we would have been here much sooner if I hadn't made so many mistakes. I'm afraid it's all my fault.'

'You must never feel badly about making mistakes,' explained Reason quietly, 'as long as you take the trouble to learn from them. For you often learn more by being wrong for the right reasons than you do by being right for the wrong reasons.'

'But there's so *much* to learn,' he said, with a thoughtful frown.

'Yes, that's true,' admitted Rhyme; 'but it's not just learn-ing things that's important. It's learning what to do with what you learn and learning why you learn things at all that matters.'

'That's just what I mean,' explained Milo, as Tock and the exhausted bug drifted quietly off to sleep. 'Many of the things I'm supposed to know seem so useless that I can't see the purpose in learning them at all.'

'You may not see it now,' said the Princess of Pure Reason, looking knowingly at Milo's puzzled face, 'but whatever we learn has a purpose and whatever we do affects everything and everyone else, if even in the tiniest way. Why, when a housefly flaps his wings, a breeze goes round the world; when a speck of dust falls to the ground, the entire planet weighs a little more; and when you stamp your foot, the earth moves slightly off its course. Whenever you laugh, gladness spreads like the ripples in a pond; and whenever you're sad, no one anywhere can be really happy. And it's much the same thing with knowledge, for whenever you learn something new, the whole world becomes that much richer.'

'And remember, also,' added the Princess of Sweet Rhyme, 'that many places you would like to see are just off the map and many things you want to know are just out of sight or a little beyond your reach. But one day you'll reach them all, for what you learn today, for no reason at all, will help you discover all the wonderful secrets of tomorrow.'

'I think I understand,' he said, still full of questions and thoughts; 'but which is the most important –'

At that moment the conversation was interrupted by a far-off chopping noise. With each loud blow, the entire room and everything in it shook and rattled. Down below, on the murky peak, the demons were busily cutting the stairway loose with axes and hammers and saws. Before long the whole thing collapsed with a tremendous crash and the startled Humbug leaped to his feet just in time to see the castle drifting slowly off into space.

'We're moving!' he shouted, which was a fact that had already become obvious to everyone.

'I think we had better leave now,' said Rhyme softly, and Reason agreed with a nod.

'But how will we get down?' groaned the Humbug, looking at the wreckage below. 'There's no stairway and we're sailing higher every minute.'

'Well, time flies, doesn't it?' asked Milo.

'On many occasions,' barked Tock, jumping eagerly to his feet. 'I'll take everyone down.'

'Can you carry us all?' inquired the bug.

'For a short distance,' said the dog thoughtfully. 'The princesses can ride on my back, Milo can catch hold of my tail, and you can hang on to his ankles.'

'But what of the Castle in the Air?' the bug objected, not very pleased with the arrangement.

'Let it drift away,' said Rhyme.

'And good riddance,' added Reason, 'for no matter how beautiful it seems, it's still nothing but a prison.'

Tock then backed up three steps and, with a running start, bounded through the window with all his passengers and began the long glide down. The princesses sat tall and unafraid, Milo held on as tightly as he could, and the bug swung crazily, like the tail on a kite. Down through the darkness they plunged, to the mountains and the monsters below.

# 19 The Return of Rhyme
and Reason

Sailing past three of the tallest peaks, and just over the outstretched arms of the grasping demons, they reached the
ground and landed with a sudden jolt.

'Quick!' urged Tock. 'Follow me! We'll have to run
for it.'

With the princesses still on his back, he galloped down the
rocky trail – and not a moment too soon. For, pounding
down the mountainside, in a cloud of clinging dust and a
chorus of chilling shrieks, came all the loathsome creatures
who choose to live in Ignorance and who had waited so very
impatiently.

Thick black clouds hung heavily overhead as they fled
through the darkness, and Milo, looking back for just a
moment, could see the awful shapes coming closer and closer.
Just to the left, and not very far away, were the Triple Demons
of Compromise – one tall and thin, one short and fat, and the
third exactly like the other two. As always, they moved in
ominous circles, for if one said 'here,' the other said 'there,'
and the third agreed perfectly with both of them. And,
since they always settled their differences by doing what none
of them really wanted, they rarely got anywhere at all – and
neither did anyone they met.

Jumping clumsily from boulder to boulder and catching

hold with his cruel, curving claws was the Horrible Hopping Hindsight, a most unpleasant fellow whose eyes were in the rear and whose rear was out in front. He invariably leaped before he looked and never cared where he was going as long as he knew why he shouldn't have gone to where he'd been.

And, most terrifying of all, directly behind, inching along like giant soft-shelled snails, with blazing eyes and wet anxious mouths, came the Gorgons of Hate and Malice, leaving a trail of slime behind them and moving much more quickly than you'd think.

'FASTER!' shouted Tock. 'They're closing in.'

Down from the heights they raced, the Humbug with one hand on his hat and the other flailing desperately in the air, Milo running as he never ran before, and the demons just a little bit faster than that.

From off on the right, his heavy bulbous body lurching dangerously on the spindly legs which barely supported him, came the Overbearing Know-it-all, talking continuously. A dismal demon who was mostly mouth, he was ready at a moment's notice to offer misinformation on any subject. And, while he often tumbled heavily, it was never he who was hurt, but, rather, the unfortunate person on whom he fell.

Next to him, but just a little behind, came the Gross Exaggeration, whose grotesque features and thoroughly unpleasant manners were hideous to see, and whose rows of wicked teeth were made only to mangle the truth. They hunted together, and were bad luck to anyone they caught.

Riding along on the back of anyone who'd carry him was the Threadbare Excuse, a small, pathetic figure whose clothes were worn and tattered and who mumbled the same things again and again, in a low but piercing voice: 'Well, I've been sick – but the page was torn out – I missed the bus – but no one *else* did it – well, I've been sick – but the page was torn out – I missed the bus – but no one *else* did it.' He looked quite harmless and friendly but, once he grabbed on, he almost never let go.

Closer and closer they came, bumping and jolting each other, clawing and snorting in their eager fury. Tock staggered along bravely with Rhyme and Reason, Milo's lungs now felt ready to burst as he stumbled down the trail, and the Humbug was slowly falling behind. Gradually the path grew broader and more flat as it reached the bottom of the mountain and turned towards Wisdom. Ahead lay light and safety – but perhaps just a bit too far away.

And down came the demons from everywhere, frenzied creatures of darkness, lurching wildly towards their prey. From off in the rear, the Terrible Trivium and the wobbly Gelatinous Giant urged them on with glee. And pounding forward with a rush came the ugly Dilemma, snorting steam and looking intently for someone to catch on the ends of his long pointed horns, while his hoofs bit eagerly at the ground.

The exhausted Humbug swayed and tottered on his rubbery legs, a look of longing on his anguished face. 'I don't think I can –' he gasped, as a jagged slash of lightning ripped open the sky and the thunder stole his words.

Closer and closer the demons loomed as the desperate chase neared its end. Then, gathering themselves for one final leap, they prepared to engulf first the bug, then the boy, and lastly the dog and his two passengers. They rose as one and –

And suddenly stopped, as if frozen in mid-air, unable to move, staring ahead in terror.

Milo slowly raised his weary head, and there on the horizon, for as far as the eye could see, stood the massed armies of Wisdom, the sun glistening from their swords and shields, and their bright banners slapping proudly at the breeze.

For a moment everything was silent. Then a thousand trumpets sounded – then a thousand more – and, like an ocean wave, the long line of horsemen advanced, slowly at first, then faster and faster, until with a gallop and a shout, which was music to Milo's ears, they swept forward towards the horrified demons.

There in the lead was King Azaz, his dazzling armour embossed with every letter in the alphabet, and, with him, the Mathemagician, brandishing a freshly sharpened staff. From his tiny wagon, Dr Dischord hurled explosion after explosion, to the delight of the Soundkeeper, while the busy DYNNE collected them almost at once. And, in honour of the occasion, Chroma the Great led his orchestra in a stirring display of patriotic colours. Everyone Milo had met during his journey had come to help – the men of the market place, the miners of Digitopolis, and all the good people from the valley and the forest.

The Spelling Bee buzzed excitedly overhead shouting, 'Charge – c-h-a-r-g-e – charge – c-h-a-r-g-e.' Canby, who, as everyone knew, was as cowardly as can be, came all the way from Conclusions to show that he was also as brave. And even Officer Shrift, mounted proudly on a long, low dachshund, galloped grimly along.

Cringing with fear, the monsters of Ignorance turned in flight and, with anguished cries too horrible ever to forget, returned to the damp, dark places from which they came. The Humbug sighed with relief, and Milo and the princesses prepared to greet the victorious army.

'Well done,' stated the Duke of Definition, dismounting and grasping Milo's hand warmly.

'Fine job,' seconded the Minister of Meaning.

'Good Work,' added the Count of Connotation.

'Congratulations,' proposed the Earl of Essence.

'CHEERS,' recommended the Under-secretary of Understanding.

And, since that's exactly what everyone felt like doing, that's exactly what everyone did.

'It's we who should thank –' began Milo, when the shouting

had subsided, but, before he could finish, they had unrolled an enormous scroll.

And, with a fanfare of trumpets and drums, they stated in order that:

'Henceforth,'
'And forthwith,'
'Let it be known by all men'
'That Rhyme and Reason'
'Reign once more in Wisdom.'

The two princesses bowed gratefully and warmly kissed their brothers, and they all agreed that a very fine thing had happened.

'And furthermore,' continued the proclamation,
'The boy named Milo,'
'The dog known as Tock,'
'And the insect hereinafter referred to as the Humbug'
'Are hereby declared to be'
'Heroes of the realm.'

Cheer after cheer filled the air, and even the bug seemed a bit embarrassed at having so much attention paid to him.

'*Therefore,*' concluded the duke, '*in honour of their glorious deed, a royal holiday is declared. Let there be parades through every city in the land and a gala carnival of three days' duration, consisting of jousts, games, feasts, and follies.*'

The five cabinet members then rolled up the large parchment and, with many bows and flourishes, retired.

Swift horsemen carried the news to every corner of the kingdom, and, as the parade slowly wound its way through the countryside, crowds of people gathered to cheer it along. Garlands of flowers hung from every house and shop and carpeted the streets. Even the air shimmered with excitement, and shutters closed for many years were thrown open to let the brilliant sunlight shine where it hadn't shone for so long.

Milo, Tock, and the very subdued Humbug sat proudly in the royal carriage with Azaz, the Mathemagician, and the two princesses; and the parade stretched for miles in both directions.

As the cheering continued, Rhyme leaned forward and touched Milo gently on the arm.

'They're shouting for you,' she said with a smile.

'But I could never have done it,' he objected, 'without everyone else's help.'

'That may be true,' said Reason gravely, 'but you had the courage to try; and what you can do is often simply a matter of what you *will* do.'

'That's why,' said Azaz, 'there was one very important thing about your quest that we couldn't discuss until you returned.'

'I remember,' said Milo eagerly. 'Tell me now.'

'It was impossible,' said the king, looking at the Mathemagician.

'Completely impossible,' said the Mathemagician, looking

at the king. 'Do you mean –' stammered the bug, who suddenly felt a bit faint.

'Yes, indeed,' they repeated together; 'but if we'd told you then, you might not have gone – and, as you've discovered, so many things are possible just as long as you don't know they're impossible.'

And for the remainder of the ride Milo didn't utter a sound.

Finally, when they'd reached a broad, flat plain midway between Dictionopolis and Digitopolis, somewhat to the right of the Valley of Sound and a little to the left of the Forest of Sight, the long line of carriages and horsemen stopped, and the great carnival began.

Gaily striped tents and pavilions sprang up everywhere as the workmen scurried about like ants. Within a few minutes there were racecourses and grandstands, side shows and refreshment booths, gaming fields, giant wheels, banners, bunting, and bedlam, almost without pause.

The Mathemagician provided a continuous display of brilliant fireworks made up of exploding numbers which multiplied and divided with breath-taking results – the colours, of course, being supplied by Chroma and the noise by a deliriously happy Dr Dischord. Thanks to the Soundkeeper, there was music and laughter and, for very brief moments, even a little silence.

Alec Bings set up an enormous telescope and invited everyone to see the other side of the moon, and the Humbug wandered through the crowd accepting congratulations and recounting in great detail his brave exploits, most of which gained immeasurably in the telling.

And each evening, just at sunset, a royal banquet was held. There was everything imaginable to eat. King Azaz had ordered a special supply of delicious words in all flavours and, for those who liked exotic foods, in all languages, too. The Mathemagician had provided innumerable platters of division

dumplings, which Milo was very careful to avoid, for, no matter how many you ate, when you finished there was more on your plate than when you began.

And, of course, following the meal came songs, epic poems, and speeches in praise of the princesses and the three gallant adventurers who had rescued them. King Azaz and the Mathemagician pledged that every year at this same time they would lead their armies to the Mountains of Ignorance until not one demon remained, and everyone agreed that no finer carnival for no finer reason had ever been held in Wisdom.

But even things as fine as all that must end sometime, and late on the afternoon of the third day the tents were struck, the pavilions were folded, and everything was packed ready to leave.

'It's time to go now,' said Reason, 'for there is much to do.'

And, as she spoke, Milo suddenly remembered his home. He wanted very much to go back, yet somehow he could not bear the thought of leaving.

'And so you must say good-bye,' said Rhyme, patting him gently on the cheek.

'To everyone?' said Milo unhappily. He looked around slowly at all the friends he'd made, and he looked very hard so as not to forget any of them for even an instant. But mostly he looked at Tock and the Humbug, with whom he had shared so much – the perils, the dangers, the fears, and, best of all, the victory. Never had anyone had two more steadfast companions.

'Can't you both come with me?' he asked, knowing the answer as he said it.

'I'm afraid not, old man,' replied the bug, 'I'd like to, but I've arranged a lecture tour which will keep me occupied for years.'

'And they do need a watchdog here,' barked Tock sadly.

Milo embraced the bug who, in his most typical fashion was heard to mumble gruffly, 'BAH,' but whose damp eyes told quite a different story. Then the boy threw his arms around Tock's neck and, for just a moment, held on very tightly.

'Thank you for everything you've taught me,' said Milo to everybody as a tear rolled down his cheek.

'And thank you for what you've taught us,' said the king – and, as he clapped his hands, the little car was brought forward, polished like new.

Milo got in and, with one last look, started down the road, with everyone waving him on.

'Good-bye,' he shouted. 'Good-bye. I'll be back.'

'Good-bye,' shouted Azaz. 'Always remember the importance of words.'

'And numbers,' added the Mathemagician forcefully.

'Surely you don't think numbers are as important as words?' he heard Azaz shout from the distance.

'Is that so?' replied the Mathemagician a little more faintly. 'Why, if –'

'Oh dear,' thought Milo; 'I do hope they don't start it all again.' And in a moment they had faded from sight as the road dipped, turned, and headed for home.

As the pleasant countryside flashed by and the wind whistled a tune on the windscreen, it suddenly occurred to Milo that he must have been gone for several weeks.

'I do hope that no one's been worried,' he thought, urging the car on faster. 'I've never been away so long before.'

The late-afternoon sun had turned now from a vivid yellow to a warm lazy orange, and it seemed almost as tired as he was. The road raced ahead in a series of gentle curves that began to look familiar, and off in the distance the solitary tollbooth appeared, a welcome sight indeed. In a few minutes he reached the end of his journey, deposited his coin, and drove through. And, almost before realizing it, he was sitting in the middle of his own room again.

'It's only six o'clock,' he observed with a yawn, and then, a moment later, he made an even more interesting discovery.

'And it's still today! I've been gone for only an hour!' he cried in amazement, for he'd certainly never realized how much he could do in so short a time.

Milo was much too tired to talk and almost too tired for dinner, so, without a murmur, he went off to bed as soon as he could. He pulled the covers around him, took a last look at his room – which somehow seemed very different than he'd remembered – and then drifted into a deep and welcome sleep.

School went very quickly the next day, but not quickly enough, for Milo's head was full of plans and his eyes could see nothing but the tollbooth and what lay beyond. He waited impatiently for the end of class, and when the time finally came, his feet raced his thoughts all the way back to the house.

'Another trip! Another trip! I'll leave immediately. They'll all be so glad to see me, and I'll –'

He stopped abruptly at the door of his room, for, where the tollbooth had been just the night before, there was now nothing at all. He searched frantically throughout the flat, but it had vanished just as mysteriously as it had come – and in its place was another bright-blue envelope, which was addressed simply: 'FOR MILO, WHO NOW KNOWS THE WAY.'

He opened it quickly and read:

Dear Milo,

You have now completed your trip, courtesy of the Phantom Tollbooth. We trust that everything has been satisfactory, and hope you understand why we have to come and collect it. You see, there are so many boys and girls waiting to use it, too.

It's true that there are many lands you've still to visit (some of which are not even on the map) and wonderful things to see (that no one has yet imagined), but we're quite sure that if you really want to, you'll find a way to reach them all by yourself.

Yours truly,

The signature was blurred and couldn't be read.

Milo walked sadly to the window and squeezed himself into one corner of the large arm-chair. He felt very lonely and desolate as his thoughts turned far away – to the foolish, lovable bug; to the comforting assurance of Tock, standing next to him; to the erratic, excitable DYNNE; to little Alec, who, he hoped, would some day reach the ground; to Rhyme and Reason, without whom Wisdom withered; and to the many, many others he would remember always.

And yet, even as he thought of all these things, he noticed somehow that the sky was a lovely shade of blue and that one cloud had the shape of a sailing ship. The tips of the trees held pale, young buds and the leaves were a rich deep green. Outside the window, there was so much to see, and hear, and touch – walks to take, hills to climb, caterpillars to watch as they strolled through the garden. There were voices to hear and conversations to listen to in wonder, and the special smell of each day.

And, in the very room in which he sat, there were books that could take you anywhere, and things to invent, and make, and build, and break, and all the puzzle and excitement of everything he didn't know – music to play, songs to sing, and worlds to imagine and then some day make real. His

thoughts darted eagerly about as everything looked new – and worth trying.

'Well, I *would* like to make another trip,' he said, jumping to his feet; 'but I really don't know when I'll have the time. There's just so much to do here.'

# The Sword in the Stone

### T. H. WHITE

Probably only the magician, Merlyn, knew that his pupil, the Wart (to rhyme with 'Art') would one day be the great King Arthur.

For six years Merlyn was the boy's tutor and the Wart learned all manner of useful things; such as what it is like to be a fish or a hawk or a badger.

Then the king, Pendragon, died without heirs. And King Pellinore arrived at the court with an extraordinary story of a sword stuck in an anvil stuck to a stone outside a church in London. Written on the sword in gold letters were the words

> *Whoso Pulleth Out This Sword of*
> *This Stone and Anvil, is Rightwise*
> *King Born of All England.*

The last person anybody expected to pull out the sword was the Wart but then he had had Merlyn as his tutor for the past six years.

# When Marnie Was There

JOAN G. ROBINSON

Brooding, lonely Anna, a foster-child, goes to stay with a kind Norfolk couple. There, like something in her memory, she finds the old house backing on to the creek. But it is the girl at the window who haunts her . . . Marnie, headstrong, often infuriating and somehow just as elusive when the two meet as she had been at the window. Marnie becomes Anna's perfect friend, and though she finally vanishes for good, she has helped Anna to make real friends.

This is a thrilling, intense story, part mystery, part adventure, part fantasy, and will appeal particularly to girls of eleven and upward.

# The Donkey Rustlers

### GERALD DURRELL

This lively story with a Greek island setting tells how Amanda and David plot to outwit the unpleasant local mayor and help their Greek friend, Yani. The villagers, and especially the mayor, depend on their donkeys for transport. If the children are to blackmail them successfully the donkeys must disappear – and disappear they do, to the consternation of the whole village . . .

Told in Gerald Durrell's dashing style with his own particular brand of humour, this story will be eagerly read by older children.

# Ghostly Experiences

## CHOSEN BY SUSAN DICKINSON

The remarkable revival of interest in ghost stories at the present time is curious, for ghost stories traditionally belong to that great age of story telling: the 19th century. And yet, despite the distractions of the television screen, ghost stories are much in demand particularly among the young. Here you will find examples of ghost stories ranging from R. L. Stevenson and J. S. LeFanu in the 19th century to the most contemporary of contemporary writers – Alan Garner and Joan Aiken.

Some of the stories are truly spine-chillers; some of the ghosts are gentle, some are not; but the collection should provide plenty of ghostly 'pleasure'.

'A splendid collection of supernatural adventures.'

*New Statesman*

'The stories in this collection have been chosen with discrimination and illustrated with a sure intuition.'

*Growing Point*